The Voice That Was in Travel

AMERICAN INDIAN LITERATURE
AND CRITICAL STUDIES SERIES

GERALD VIZENOR AND LOUIS OWENS,
GENERAL EDITORS

Other Books by Diane Glancy

NOVELS

The Only Piece of Furniture in the House (Wakefield, R.I., 1996)
Pushing the Bear: A Novel of the Trail of Tears (New York, 1996, 1998)
Flutie (Wakefield, R.I., 1998)

SHORT STORIES

Trigger Dance (Normal, Ill., 1990; Frankfurt, Germany, 1995)
Firesticks: A Collection of Stories (Norman, 1993)
Monkey Secret (Evanston, 1995)

POETRY

One Age in a Dream (Minneapolis, 1986)
Offering (Duluth, 1988)
Iron Woman (Minneapolis, 1990)
Lone Dog's Winter Count (Albuquerque, 1991)
Boom Town (Goodhue, Minn., 1997)
Primer of the Obsolete (Tucson, 1998)

DRAMA

War Cries, A Collection of Nine Plays (Duluth, 1996)

ANTHOLOGIES

(editor, with David Mura, Juanita Garciagodoy, and Musa Moore-
Foster) *Braided Lives, An Anthology of Multicultural American
Writing* (St. Paul, 1991)
(editor, with Bill Truesdale) *Two Worlds Walking: Anthology of Mixed
Heritage Writings* (Minneapolis, 1994)
(editor, with Mark Nowak) *Visit Teepee Town: Native Writings after the
Detours* (Minneapolis, 1999)

NONFICTION

Claiming Breath (Lincoln, 1992)
The West Pole (Minneapolis, 1997)
The Cold-and-Hunger Dance (Lincoln, 1998)

The Voice That Was in Travel
Stories

Diane Glancy

University of Oklahoma Press : Norman

Library of Congress Cataloging-in-Publication Data

Glancy, Diane.
   The voice that was in travel : stories / Diane Glancy.
      p.   cm. — (American Indian literature and critical studies
   series ; v. 33)
      ISBN 0-8061-3157-8 (cloth : alk. paper)
      1. United States—Social life and customs—20th century Fiction.
   2. Americans—Travel—Foreign countries Fiction.   3. Indians of
   North America Fiction.   4. Voyages and travels.   I. Title.
   II. Series.
   PS3557.L294V64   1999
   813'.54—dc21   99-21329
                                                         CIP

The Voice That Was in Travel: Stories is Volume 33 in the American Indian Literature and Critical Studies Series.

The paper in this book meets the guidelines for permanence and durability of the Committee on Production Guidelines for Book Longevity of the Council on Library Resources, Inc. ∞

Text design by Gail Carter.

Contents

Preface

I remember seeing cars with decals on the windows from travels to different states. As a child, in the middle of the country, I wanted to go to all those places. In passing, I think I have used that memory to place these stories as decals on a car window from travels in South Dakota, Oklahoma, Missouri, Arkansas, Germany, Italy, Australia—all the places I eventually got to. Imaginary landscapes also. Even the landscapes between the placement of the stories to one another. Their *junto / jackstraw* relationship.

The stories migrate between connectives and *disconnectives*. Sometimes with disrupted syntax torn in places. Sentences sometimes shortened to a few words. Sometimes without a verb. Sometimes run on.

In a previous collection, *Firesticks*, number 5 in the American Indian Literature and Critical Studies Series, I *stranded* creative nonfiction, narratives, short stories, and a novella. I also sliced the sections of the novella between the stories and creative nonfictions. I wanted to reflect the broken context of native life. A heritage nearly erased in places. *Firesticks*, the words that travel between genres, between places like headlights on a dark road, are the unifying force.

In this collection, the light from the *firesticks* comes from the frictions between silence and *voicings*. The jaunty excursions into variable perspectives. The erosion of actual experience into moving emblems of realizations.

Acknowledgments

The following stories have been previously published: "Reaching for Air," in *Architrave* (1996); "Badlands," in *The Carolina Quarterly* 50, no. 1 (1997); "Road," in *Westview, A Journal of Western Oklahoma* (1995), and *Minnesota Writers Collection* (Madison, Wis.: Crowbar Press, 1995); "The Birds with the Breeze of Their Wings," in *Sgraffito* (1996); "A Later Game of Marbles," with the title, "Landscape Painting," in *Two Worlds Walking: Anthology of Mixed Heritage Writings*, edited by Bill Truesdale and Diane Glancy (Minneapolis: New Rivers Press, 1998); "Crossing the Specific," in *What Is Not Said*, edited by Ricardo Cortez Cruz, Fiction Collective 2, Southern Illinois University; "In the Burrito," in *The Talking of Hands*, edited by Robert Alexander, Mark Vinz, and Bill Truesdale (Minneapolis: New Rivers Press, 1998); "You Know Those People Don't Talk," in *Prairie Schooner* (1994); "The Man Whose Voice Was in Travel," in *Fuel* (1995); "The Great House," in *Iowa Woman* (1996); "A Woman Who Sewed for Me a Dress That Sleeves Didn't Fit," in *The American Voice* 39 (1996); "There He Is Again," in *Windhover* 2, no. 1 (1998); and "America's First Parade," in *Cimarron Review* 121 (1997).

I am grateful to the following sources for materials used in "America's First Parade": Ralph E. Dawson III and Shirley Dawson, *Cherokee-English Interlinear First Epistle of John*, Rocky Ford Project, Church of Christ, Moody, Oklahoma, for section 16; Chris Maynard and Bill Scheller, *Manifold Destiny* (New York: Random House, 1988), for the recipe for "Poached Fish Pontiac" in section 19; and the *Indian Pioneer Papers, WPA*

Biographies, Western History Collections, University of Oklahoma, Norman, for some of the details remembered on grandma's place.

I am also indebted to the USIS, the Jerome Foundation, the Loft, and various other travel grants and fellowships for the stories, some of them *clipped,* which I picked up in the peripheral fields along the road.

The Voice That Was in Travel

*Give me stories
that* hiz like farworks.

UNCLE SNOWBALL

*The kingdom of God is like a man
traveling into a far country.*

MATTHEW 25:14

*Pies para que lost quiero,
si tengo alas pa'volar.*

FRIDA KAHLO

Reaching for Air

> *In the six hundredth year of Noah's life, in the*
> *second month, the seventeenth day of the month,*
> *the same day were all the fountains of the great deep*
> *broken up, and the windows of heaven were opened.*
>
> GENESIS 7:11

It's hard to wake in a foreign country after an all-night cross-Atlantic flight and find your way to the breakfast room. The Japanese / Germans know you are not them in your awkwardness, the garish violence of your ways, they see you are American. The eggs / bacon / toast / the tin you take thinking it's jam, but it's farm liver sausage. *Landleberwerst.* You know it at the table with your glasses on. And later you find the jelly pot when you go back for cereal and yogurt which you pour into a small bowl and carry to your table with a large spoon for Americans who are all mouthed and no eared.

You don't look up but you feel their eyes. You know their derision as you eat your breakfast you ask for coffee. The woman brings it you know you should have gotten it from the serving table yourself. There's a limitless amount of things you can do in a foreign country to prove you're American.

And you wish there was a glass of water on the table as you read your book. You don't look at them when you look up you see the plates of meats and cheeses and fruits the pink napkins. The dreams of horror and violence that staked the night. The glass of water you don't have. Its clarity and transparency letting what is behind it through yet distorting it. An observation you make in a country where they shape you

3

with their ideas, where they bump you with their language you don't understand.

You're a middle-aged, mixblood woman alone in a foreign country on a U.S. Information Service tour. Your companion's back in the states in MN in St. Paul in his house on Exeter Place with its disheveled papers while all the world in Europe in Germany in Hannover in the Hotel Mussman is orderly and tidy and predictable as your own German mother's eruptions over your messiness when you were growing up.

But it turns out the fractures of your heritage, your mess and the struggle to get through it, made stories you travel to read. There is even a fullness, a volume, you feels sometimes in the difficulties of your life. Even when it frightens you.

Sometimes you find your jet lag lets you see into the cut of your dreams as they happen. You feel yourself crawl along the wall. Your arms held to your chest your head whacked off you see it roll up the street.

Somewhere you hear the noise.

You feel the heat of your body, the itch in your ears, the faulty heartbeat that knocked your chest like the fist on the door when you overslept. Those thick comforters on the narrow beds that won't let your body heat escape. The huge pillow that pushes your chin to your chest.

You remember how the shape of night held your dreams when you were not asleep. After you went off in their blackness following a truck closed in.

From your window you see pigeons on the square, the rain, the people hurrying from the station across the square, the flags violent on their posts. The woman still in your room. The noise of her vacuum cleaner a plane coming down on your head. While she works you open the *Gidenbunk* Bible. *Bruder matthaus kepiter 1:2. Abraham zeugte Isaak. Isaak zeugte Juda und Seine.* You turn the Bible backward to the *flut.*

As she cleans you read names in the telephone book. *Sabine. Margot. Willi. Manfrit. Jutta.*

Another truck with a loud motor passes in the street.

Later they come into your room without knocking to check the drapes if they're raised to their certain place. They turn off the light as if you were not reading, because you're an American they think you're wasteful.

You give your first reading on the USIS tour. You answer questions about walking in the white and Indian worlds. The lecture hall's utilitarian and packed with students. Afterwards you return to the hotel. You pack your clothes, you pull your luggage down the hall through the doors between the halls, the cramped elevator, its doors again and stairs. You take the train, the tight passage between compartments.

In open country you watch the rolling fields through northern Germany in the time of *flut*. You watch the little sandbagged and levied towns. Freed from your own classes for a week. Your stacks of papers to grade.

The women with baby carriages with bundles and umbrellas, the men in raincoats, the students with backpacks as you ride backward through the country you pass a farmer's row of bee boxes. How swift the backward travel seeing where you've been not what's happened until it passes.

The quaint old stone streets the narrow tall row houses as if someone said, *move closer*, til you passed.

Maybe you adjust because you live behind a bakery in St. Paul and they wake you in the night loading trucks and then you sleep again or go without a lot of sleep and this is more of it.

Maybe you've always known what it is to move on.

From Hannover to Bremen to Kiel. You see the line of fenceposts through the fields of water as if the world between floods was spinning. You nod during the train's smooth ride over tracks rocking the waters. You remember the animals you

5

saw in the tourist shop in Bremen, the one day flooding the next.

Kuh.

Schwein.

Pferd.

Huhn.

Hund.

You wrote their names on paper. You think of them again when you see fence posts walking single file through the water. An ark maybe somewhere in the fields.

You ride your dreams happening while you watch them moving swiftly over water.

You open the ark of your mouth. You speak a dry place.

Cow.

Pig.

Horse.

Hen.

Dog.

You're in a place trying to recover from its history as you're trying to recover from you own, and you see the edges of the fields you turned like posters where you stopped between planes in Amsterdam.

You went to the museum hurrying on a trolley through the city. Asking directions when you got off. Upstairs you saw the greenish garishness of Van Gogh's sunflowers. Their claws and maned heads. You saw their beaks. The crows in them. The images of crows and lions intertwined as tares in the wheatfield. Before you hurried back to the airport.

Sometimes you wake in the foreign country of your head. You sort through jelly jars and milk cans. The barns lined up like barracks. You hear the shrieks of stalks. The sunflowers beating the train through a story. The real and the facsimile you have in your head.

Sometimes between stops you see the holes in the sky. You hear the noise of someone you think in traffic. Maybe Abraham and Isaac. Jacob and Esau. But you're in the time of flood now. Maybe Noah and his wife sweeping animals into the ark.

You feel your struggle your overload of work, the weight of the air on your shoulders. You have a companion back in St. Paul who'll show up as long as you cook for him. Who'll show up as long as you make him comfortable. But your companion's not going to marry you. You know it. You even accept it and you're grateful for his companionship.

You have an academic position. You're on tenure track. You attend the department meetings. Do the work no one else wants. You're plain and alone and you have to survive. You're someone who will work. Will bear up. You know your blessings of simplicity and striving.

You think of the courage of life. You see it everywhere you travel. You pick it up from the towns where the train passes. You don't give up.

Sometimes everything feels *jumped up*. The land bearing more water than it usually would. The people looking from the passing train.

Sometimes you hear your dreams. The changing boundaries of violence and ease. It's the place you're from. The stops you make between wakings.

You hear the absolute you read from the act of your making. Sometimes you see right through the waters to the amplitude of heaven.

Blast

Sometimes the furnace lit with a boom. Mada could feel the floor shake. Somewhere there was a buildup of gas.

She was eating Christmas cookies green as winter grass until her tongue was green, she felt it again. You know you can bring a federal bldg to its knees with fertilizer and a truck.

Mada called the furnace man who said nothing was wrong.

Everytime she heard aftershocks on winter nights she dreamed the furnace in the basement would burn their beds.

She called the furnace man again he said this time he fixed it. But still it boomed sometimes when it lit.

She lived in a world that needed fixing, that was filled with booms no one seemed to know how to fix.

She knew when the house grew cold just before the furnace turned on she was living the edge of existence she was living a blast.

Badlands

Forecast—Nothing ever felt like This.
Forecast—Hound Dog.

Forecast—The Incidents may presage war.
Forecast—I am my love—a Lucky girl.

LUCIE BROCK-BROIDO
"Prescient," *The Master Letters*

She came like a piece of lightning. She said, "We're taking our broken-down horse of a school bus from Pine Ridge to Pierre. We're driving a hundred miles next month. We're going to debate. Now, let's prepare. Men of war. Women warriors. Our voice will be in travel. Who's the best speaker in class?"

"No one."

"Go to the library. Look up Venice."

"We don't have a book with Venice in it."

"One of you girls, find a book with somewhere in it. Pretend you've been there and give the most stuck-up speech you've ever given. Until you don't even like yourself."

"We got encyclopedias in the library someone sent us. They're older than the Badlands."

The debate teacher said, "we're going to feel like we can't do anything. Get used to it. It's the way we'll always feel against them. We can't put a sentence together. We can't hold a straight thought. We just talk in clumps.

"Now you other girls. Wear no makeup. But the one speaking about Venice will take half an hour in the girl's room putting on her makeup. She'll wear a *Miss Indian America* crown. She'll wear a Pierre red prom dress I'm going to get somewhere. She'll come into the room.

"Boys, you fall over yourselves. And you plain girls, give a speech about the Badlands and tell us about it without lipstick or anything on your face so you'll feel like the worst enemy of yourself.

"I want you to hate yourselves in front of the girl with all the makeup. I want you to feel your stupid speeches. And boys, you talk while the girls are in the middle of the Badlands, or look at the pretty girl who's not even talking, until the plain girls feel like nothing. Until they feel like an Indian. You plain girls, wear the oldest thing you like least."

"I got a closet full."

"Well, put them on. We're going on a practice run."

They looked at one another when she left the room.

Where had she come from? Without a husband or boyfriend. Living at the end of a dirt road in a house that was abandoned. There was talk she was a widow. Her husband had died young.

There was talk she was a witch. Maybe a medicine woman. Someone said they'd seen her standing at the end of the road at night. Her arms raised to the air. The stars fancy-dancing over her head.

But no one knew anything for sure.

A few days later, she put the plain girls on the bus and drove them from Pine Ridge through Mission, South Dakota, with the windows down, and got them back to school. The kids in the halls were all talking and staring at them and ignoring them in alternate situations.

The hall bell was ringing as if there were a fire drill, and she called them this way, then that, through the halls of their school that looked like a battle zone. Past a glass case with two old trophys.

The kids watching laughed at their confusion.

She lead them in one room, changed her mind, and hurried them down the hall to another room. She told them the girl in the red dress was speaking in the next room, and she was going to listen to her. The plain girls sat in the room by themselves, not knowing what to do or when the debate teacher would come back for them.

She left them waiting by themselves until the next room, where the girl spoke about Venice, broke out in clapping, as though the girl in the red dress were terrific and on a high ground they'd never achieve, and would always feel their shame and humiliation, and whatever they did, they would always be nothing. And they'd be pounded into the ground and that was all they'd ever be. Just stumps.

They might as well stay on the reservation and drink themselves under one of those white crosses along the roads.

And she brought the girl in the red dress into the room. She was the best speaker in the debate tournament, and wasn't she pretty? The debate teacher decided she would give her speech on Venice again. The boys that had followed her into the room fell over themselves as the pretty girl talked about the streets of water and the boats gliding over them like eagles on a high summer sky.

The boys clapped and stood when she finished. While they were still cheering, the debate teacher turned to one of the plain girls and said, "It's your turn to speak."

And the plain girl got up and stammered about the Badlands and how the wind ate the earth, and the boys still looked at the girl in the red dress.

"The Dakota name for the Badlands is *Maka Sicha*," the plain girl said. "It was eroded by wind and the White River. The sawtooth plateaus are a result of rocks of varying resistence. Layers of shale, for instance, were washed from between harder layers of limestone and conglomerates."

When the plain girl finished talking, the boys hardly noticed.

The next plain girl spoke about the Oligocene fossil beds in the Badlands. The remains of mammals from 30 million years ago. Horse, camel, rhinoceros, dog, cat, tapir, deer, rodent, turtle, crocodile, and birds which were now extinct.

The next plain girl said that animals are scarce in the Badlands. Maybe there's rabbit, gopher, prairie dog, mouse, snake, coyote. But there wouldn't be much hunting. None of them had been to the Badlands, though it wasn't that far away. She said her uncle knew someone who'd been.

When she finished, the boys still looked at the girl in the red dress.

The debate teacher said, "Next week we're going to do the same to the boys.

We're going to work on a conglomerate of our stories after that."

And if they learned to do it that way, they could go to debates and speech tournaments. They could bear the shame of arriving in their bus, which was held together by a medicine song and a prayer.

"Just think of them. They come to pollute our water and land. They come to destroy our self-image. That's how they plan to get rid of us. But we're going to be strong through ceremony. Through faith.

In going, our voice will come."

Next month, after the boys had their turn being snubbed by the girls, and after they worked through a story that carried all their voices, they drove a hundred miles with the wind and dust blowing through the bus. The debate teacher held to the steering wheel as if it were a broom, her witch-black hair whipping her neck.

They pulled up in the large parking lot of the Pierre high school. They saw the Greyhound buses from other South Dakota schools.

Yes, there were the enemies. The destroyers. Immature and not yet powerful. But they'd have it. Yes, someday.

The Indian students filed off their old bus. They wanted to run. Their shame would have fried an egg on their face. They felt surrounded, hated. They could not speak a word. Their debate teacher smiled at them. She didn't say anything.

The school in Pierre was new. Inside, the desks were shiny and huge. The floors polished. The trophy cases spilling with triumph.

The Indian students shriveled together.

It was someone's turn to speak from another school, and then another from still another school. The Indian students shrank into themselves. The girl, especially, who'd worn the red dress, seemed terrorized more than the others.

When it was their turn to speak, one plain girl got up and walked to the front of the classroom. The others got up and went with her. Because it was their way.

"*Maka Sicha*. The Badlands."

She told their conglomerate story as the Indian students stood awkwardly in front of the debate students from other schools.

"In southwestern South Dakota, the earth is eaten into as if a bone a dog had chewed. One ridge then another and the land is marked by the teeth of a dog sinking into it. There's an ugliness. A strangeness. You feel it in your mouth.

Because the Badlands is a place without a story. It's what happens when you forget the words of your stories."

The students that stood with the girl looked at the ceiling as she talked. They looked at the floor when she said the particular words they had given to the speech.

"But when the sun comes through the dust, just before dark, there's a haze. You can see the ghost dance of gondolas with their flags rippling the wind. You can see the streets of water in the Badlands. Only those who remember their stories can see.

Because the Badlands didn't have a story of its own. It was given to us so we might remember what it's like to forget our stories. To forget we are made of sound. The land was eaten as if a bone. But our words fill the gullies and valleys with water. Our words are the boats that float there. Behind our words, you can hear the little striped flags beating in the wind. A color for each direction. Black. Red. Yellow. White."

Parachute Rocket w/ Flare

Ozmo loved fireworks. He said their names over and over.
Mag missiles.
Black box artillery.
Smoke grenades.
Tanks.
B-3 bombers w/ report.
Saturn missile batteries.
Ozark M-8 smoke.
Phoenix tail howls.
Ozmo took his first breath.
Cloud dragons.
Magic whips.
Whistling bottle rockets.
Cuckoos.
Killer bees.
Silver shock waves.
Wild geese.
Thunderstorms.
Wooh. Those crackers had a ping.

Ozmo housed his pyrotechnic company, called *Great Balls of Fire*, in Jerusalem, Arkansas. He drove across Highway 124 to Russellville. They were sponsoring a patriotic *portamento.* There was no one else but Ozmo to forecast the show. Sometimes they called him the *Arkansas Volcano.* He honked his horn with the precision of shooting fireworks over the thick highway through the woods. On the dash, he patted his plastic Marco Polo, who'd brought the first fireworks from

China. He patted the map of the Bering Strait, where his Indian ancestors had crossed to this continent. That's how they went together. His ancestors and the fireworks from China.

Yes. Russellville wanted to hear what Ozmo had at his fireworks stand. Just the firecracker up his airway, Ozmo thought as he drove from Jerusalem to Russellville.

He was more than a fireworks stand. Ozmo was the voice of fireworks itself. He ordered from the factory in Oklahoma. Last summer they'd had an explosion. A crate pushed along the loading dock sparked a box of crackers and for some it was July Fourth forever. The whole place gone up. He'd driven to Hallet, Oklahoma, across the glass mountains to the funeral. Ozmo wiped his eyes and the men looked at one another.

Ozmo found an alternate supplier in Tennessee. It was just more inconvenient.

Ozmo ate his fireballs and buzz bombs. His head did a spin up. He swore the trees twirled. He didn't know which way he spoke. Ozmo had to get a grip on himself he thought as he drove. He couldn't let his mind wander or what would they do without him in Russellville?

Mammoth smoke.

Four seasons.

Burglar alarms.

Bang matches.

Cigarette loads.

What a portfolio.

Ozmo—the man at the head table said. But Ozmo talked on. For the men we got the *Whistling wheels.*

For the ladies we got the dainties.

Chrysanthemums.

Camelias.

Moon flitters.

Hen laying eggs.

Swarming butterflies.

Even your little fireflowers needed a *jumping frog* now and then. Unless they were fizzlers, he chuckled to himself.

Ozmo—the man at the head table leaned forward.

The others looked at their watches. They had to get back to work. They had to get on with their day. The patriotic *portamento* and all.

Ozmo was making stories. He was making truth with his words. When he was a boy they said a giant firecracker scared him. The flying sparks zoned him into the hereafter. The here to now. Alternating weeping and laughter.

He was still up there with them. Ozmo loved the smell. Once you had it in your nose you'd never blow it out. He loved the movable boundaries. The unpredictable realities. The possibilities exploding. The ladies would squeak with delight. The *works* had an effect on women. Ozmo was in orbit. They knew it now.

Cherry smoke balls.

Blue comets.

Willows.

Morning glory sparkers.

Festival balls.

Ozmo wanted to see them continuous in the sky. Playing to one another. He could almost hear the trombones of their yellows. The fiddles of their reds. The juice harp of their russets. *Wuuh!* Arlyle, Ozmo's wife, had an Uncle Snowball who played the saw.

Think what we did as boys. Took the heads right off grasshoppers. Remember how we tied insects to bottle rockets and sent them to space? Think what would lift.

Ozmo dreamed firecrackers. His wife Arlyle could make sounds like *Killer bees* and *Phoenix tails*. Sometimes she whizzled him to sleep.

The men talked at their tables. When would the man at the head table inform Ozmo he was half a year behind in their afternoon?

Jumping jacks.

Fun snappers.

Piggy wigglers.

That's treading air right there in the night.

While the lady artist with the big earrings and the hair across her eyebrows, Ozmo said—as if her brows didn't want to be apart and joined hands over her nose.

The man at the head table cleared his watch. Yes. Ozmo was now in his second lifetime and wasting theirs. How could they get him to sit down? It was a quarter to two.

They had asked for a simple several minutes at most. Would he talk until July Fourth?

Even the day wasn't enough to hold Ozmo's words about fireworks. They spilled into the night. His wife, Arlyle, would wake with the sound of his voice. Usually she'd catch phrases of rockets and whizzers. Sometimes she'd hear *Wiggy Piglers.* Or she'd hear the tiny explosions from fireworks far away in his sleep. Or the ancestors on the trail across the Bering Strait.

Ozmo—she'd say. *Ozmo*— And she'd put her hand over his mouth before he started to roar. Otherwise, he'd light up a *Cloud dragon* and she'd see his eyes rise under his lids.

Other times she'd hear him clearly in the night. He'd talk through the whole process— *Lifting charge. Time fuse. Stars and pellets. Aluminum flakes. Black powder. Sulfur. Potassium chlorate.* The day was coming when Ozmo would assemble his own fireworks. Arlyle saw it now. He'd already asked Uncle Snowball to play his saw when he planned his fireworks shows. He was already wanting to customize some of the fireworks he bought. How long before she'd see him caked with black powder and aluminum flakes?

Yes. Ozmo was combustible.

Fireworks were the sheep of his pasture. Fireworks were his prayers.

They could write him at:

Ozmo's Great Balls of Far

Rought 1

Jerusalem, AR 72080

He was known everywhere. He'd traveled to Imboden and Judsonia, even Pocahontas in the northeast corner. Arlyle's Uncle Snowball went with him sometimes. He was the detonator.

Ozmo saw the year as a wheel with July Fourth on top. The other months moved toward it or away from it. Yes, July Fourth was the pinnacle. In autumn, the earth was lit with the flames of red and yellow leaves. In winter, the woodsmoke had the smell of firecrackers. The snow, the few times it fell in Arkansas, was the ash and fallout from last summer's fireworks. Then the earth was full of *Ground bloomers* on its way to the Fourth again.

Ozmo envisioned the afterworld as a ballistic display. He could see God with a fuse in his mouth.

OZMO—the man at the head table insisted—

Fireworks encapsulated the gross energies of the sun. The elemental forces of the solar system all sacked up in bright tissue-thin papers.

Yes, fireworks sent you up. Took you across the Milky Way. *Ka-smoozo!* Ozmo could blow anything to *smithereens*.

Maybe they'd have to tie Ozmo to a *Parachute rocket*.

Ozmo saw their faces ready to ignite. The Russellville leaders were with him now. He could open up space to an interstellar whizz show. It was something like revenge.

But the man at the head table stood—he moved toward Ozmo like a *Silver twinkler*. It seemed the others were *Black snakes*.

19

Ozmo could face the multiplicity of possibilities. He could extrapolate the universe. He could give them an act of the imagination as an alternative to his bursts of grief—as a substitute for the crying that followed his laughter.

Ozmo was talking about bunkers. Storehouses. He was ready for the *intergalactic* when he felt himself ushered to the door—

Zondede— Ozmo cracked as he drove back to Jerusalem, Arkansas. His firecracker truck with cab lights and mud flaps sizzling in takeoff. His heart exploding into a million parts. *Zumboto*. Ozmo honked at being launched. He honked at being sent adrift with only the gravity of the earth to pull him back.

The low sun flashed from a pond like a Mag missile.

Booming tubas.

Yes. They had enjoyed that one.

Road

Carleen was on the road all the time. She couldn't stop traveling. She had to feel the land passing under her. She had one daughter with a sick child. Another daughter without a job. She had to keep moving between them. She could talk to her companion on the phone. How could they be close when she was always gone? He would ask. Well, she had to keep traveling and he couldn't always follow.

The road pulled against the hard things she had to pull against. The twenty-pound turkey her one daughter had bought when there were just the four of them and one was the sick child. She'd thawed the frozen bird in the bathtub in cold water all night. Her daughter's sink in the kitchen was not deep enough to cover it. She remembered her daughter's frustration and impatience. Her temper at being constrained in a small box of a life. She wanted to kick against the walls of the apartment. Knock it down. Start over.

She had felt a tearing in herself as she worked in the kitchen with her daughter. She was angry because she'd worked hard to sew her life together and her daughters' problems were pulling at the stitches.

When was she coming back? He asked on the phone.

Carleen remembered she'd watched television as she talked to her companion. Switching back and forth between the channels. There'd been a drought in Australia. Another drought in Africa. She remembered the kangaroo running. There were brush fires in the Blue Mountains in Australia near Sydney. Then she watched a baby elephant in Africa who couldn't stand.

I thought the lions were going to eat him, she said on the phone.

She remembered the mother tossing him with her foot to get him to stand. But the little elephant couldn't stand. He had tried pathetically to follow the herd, walking on the knees of his front legs. Not even able to reach his mother to nurse.

Carleen loved calling him her boyfriend. They were both grandparents. Their lives were established, yet there was that longing for companionship, for otherness. But their lives were separate. She was always traveling. Oklahoma to Missouri to Kansas to Oklahoma. Listening to the gospel on the radio. She went to church while he was content to read the Sunday paper and say he'd like to go. Maybe someday he would go, but for now she went to church by herself.

There'd been another calf born. Was it Australia? Africa? He was hardly breathing in the hot sun. She remembered the drought again when she talked to her boyfriend from the road. The mother had lifted him in the air in her trunk and carried him above her head to the shade of a scraggly bush.

Then there'd been another elephant in labor. Her thin tail high in the air as she stepped backwards. She wouldn't go near her baby when it was born and another elephant removed the sack. Still another elephant touched the stillborn calf with her back feet in an elephant ceremony, kicking up the ground as if searching for roots in drought.

The little elephant who couldn't stand was bigger than any calf the commentator had seen. He'd been cramped in the womb with his legs under him. He couldn't straighten his front legs. He'd rub his knees raw trying to walk that way and they'd get infected. And the little elephant still couldn't stand. He'd still fall over when he'd try to reach his mother for her milk.

But wildlife regulations and objectivism prevented the commentator or the park officials from doing anything.

Carleen had looked away from the television. It reminded her of her daughter's child. The burning African fever she'd felt when she held her. Her daughters' father had come. Her former husband who'd left them stranded. She'd been in church when she heard a minister read about Lot, who offered his daughters to the crowd instead of the men they wanted. But the men were really angels who only looked like men. They had come to tell Lot that Sodom would be destroyed. Lot gave them lodging in his house for the night and the Sodomites came asking for them. Lot had offered his daughters instead. How could he? The angels could take care of themselves. But she knew a man could give his family away.

Then there'd been a fire. She said to her boyfriend on the phone when they talked again. Just like in Australia. The grasses crackled. Maybe the whole continent would burn. The animal herds stampeded. A lizard climbed a branch.

She wasn't one for observation. She would have gotten in there and kicked dust. She would have gotten in there and prayed.

She passed a shed on its knees like the little elephant. A thicket of bright yellow leaves. A thin dog walking beside the highway. A flock of geese. A splatter of birds.

Yes, on the road Carleen was in the outback. She was in the jungle. She was on a safari of fast-moving cars. She was driving around the world. Crossing oceans. Switching between her daughters as if they were television programs. She loved the migration over the land. It gave her a chance to think. To get away. To get perspective. To see where she was going.

She remembered the intelligent look in her daughters' eyes, but they hadn't developed their intelligence. Or their faith. It was there. It was just something they weren't using. Was it something she hadn't done?

For now, her daughter seemed remote and in one place. Not yet loose. Maybe it was the dullness of her marriage and the no-way-out life she lived. The demands of the sick child. An uncaring husband and father of her daughters.

Her own father had also traveled. How often had he been gone? How he had wanted to fly. Then she'd had a husband who was the same. Did everyone want to be away from her? She'd had a relationship since her divorce many years ago. She'd had several relationships. But she felt that final life with someone wouldn't happen. That final man would not come into her life.

She had an aging aunt who'd been together with her husband over fifty years. It was strange how some people came into the world in pairs. They only had to spend a few years of childhood on their own and then they were with their mate all their lives. They only had to meet one another. They were so much like one person you knew when one died the other wouldn't be far behind. Following into the beyond.

In her aunt and uncle's house there was order. The last time she was there, the glasses for company had been unwrapped and boxed again with the cardboard sections. Everything was in its place.

They could wait all day to read their paper because they had such generous amounts of time. She had to grab what would be hers.

She felt their little vacuum she carried with her in the car. The ticking clock in their house. The quietness. The turning of a page. The cathedral cookies and divinity her aunt made, her cane hanging over the chair.

The morning sun was brilliant on the clouds. The geese and the sprinkle of birds in the clouded sky. The usual autumn when the cold mornings caused the sap to rise. Isn't that what made some leaves turn red and yellow and others a shiny brown as if they were made of iron and rusted in the damp autumn mornings?

What would Africa be like in frost?

She heard a pebble thrown up on the windshield. A truck passed on the interstate and she picked up speed to follow. A Batesville Casket Company truck. She passed some farmhouses, a flash of cattle, the lovely air.

There was a band of sky through the clouds. Sometimes she'd be thinking and the time would travel. Other times it took forever. A mile was a long way. And she traveled hundreds. She put her blinker on and passed another car.

There was a harvester with a long nose in a field. She remembered the lizard crawling up a branch to get away from the fire. Her legs felt hot and she turned down the heat.

The spitting fire of the African grasses. She was that lizard clinging to a branch. She was the elephant on her knees. Isn't that what living did? With its tongue of fire. Its cramped situations. She had gotten singed. She had gotten burned. Her daughter was in line for the same.

Her former husband had come to her daughter's apartment looking like he'd been to the Australian outback. How much had his jacket cost? How much had he withheld from them? The lawyer she got once had cost her more than the court had awarded her. Then her daughters had turned eighteen and his meager payments were over.

He'd hardly looked at his sick grandchild. His daughter made him a turkey sandwich and he ate in the other room. Away from her, his former wife. Why had he even come? He only stirred up old ground. She could take him between her hands. Tell him she was more of a man. She could rip off his jacket and wear it herself. She could ash him with her words.

But it was in church she had dumped her anger. It was in prayer she had spoken her hostility. The unfairness of it all.

In their prayer meetings at church, there had been other women who cried, still in love with their husbands. At least she was over that. Yes, she could crawl up his arm like a lizard. She could eat his eyes.

Faith was a companion more than her husband had been. Faith was more than her boyfriend. It was faith that held her like the sun coming up on another field. The cornstalks in the field with their arms lifted as if asking the sky to pick them up.

Carleen heard the men talk about their anger also. Sometimes it worked both ways. They didn't always get off either.

They were all like the little elephant with his tendons not stretched, walking on their knees. But the elephant had finally stood and nudged his mother for milk. She had thought, watching television, he'd probably die from the lions. She had felt every effort he made. Probably her son-in-law had noticed how intensely she watched the program. But she had struggled like the elephant. Holding the pillow to her chest in her daughter's small apartment. It was what she had found out. She would have to bow her knees before God to get anywhere. That's why she had knees, so they'd bend. That's why she liked driving. It kept her knees bent.

But she knew her own. Didn't the elephants know their own bones and when they found them they had a ceremony? She thought about her daughter who had a daughter who'd have a daughter who'd have. Weren't they bound together?

She was full of bitter memories and expectations at the same time. She'd had a husband who had let her down. A boyfriend who wasn't as adventurous as she was. Two daughters who were locked in frustration. An aunt and uncle facing old age and death. A television which could jump all over the world. A minister who said God's love rested on them all. A God who understood their ambiguity and hurt. The contradictions and complexities of their humanness.

She'd thought about her boyfriend that night she'd slept on her daughter's couch. After her son-in-law had gone to bed. Wakened at times by the child.

Carleen felt brittle as leaves about to fall. Maybe she'd walk only a short time in the history of the upright, then return to her bed like an old aunt or a sick child. And her spirit would separate to her maker like the interchanges on the highway. The forks in the road. The bypasses.

She drove on the highway and saw the cattails along the ditches. The thickets along the fences. The farmhouses. The crowd of cows in the harvested cornrows. Fields. Pastures. The flock of birds. The spattering of geese. The sky.

It wasn't that her boyfriend didn't want to go with her, but there was something missing in their relationship that she thought about and he didn't when their brittle bones embraced.

She wondered what she'd do with her aging aunt. They had no children. After her parent's death, they thought she was their child. She was glad the road was between them. She felt choppy as the surface of a lake she passed.

Was she becoming a man as she aged? She could keep up with them on the highway. She could drive with them after dark and keep going, rise early, move on. She could be part of the momentum of migration over the land. Not some wiggler over the road.

But why did she define that independent part of herself as a man? Her ability to drive. Her willfulness. Her self-centeredness. It was what she'd seen in men. She wasn't going to move over and make room for someone. She didn't have the patience to start over. To do all that again. Maybe she was becoming like the former husband she didn't like.

Maybe she could see her anger and strength as part of her womanliness. She had not discarded her caring for others. She felt her gentleness. Religion.

Where the divided highway was separated by some distance, the oncoming traffic moved like farmhouses along the road.

But it was a man's voice that emerged from her now as she traveled. She was her own friend. Women were women for a while, then the man in them took the wheel.

Soon she'd stop for gas and call her boyfriend again from the road and they'd talk and there'd be that closeness she longed for. But when it came to down to it, he would stay in his house and she would stay in hers. She'd still be on the road alone. The oneness of her aunt and uncle would not be hers. When she put her hand in her glove on a cold morning, it was her own glove she put her hand into. It was herself she fit into.

Carleen would have to be satisfied. Otherwise. If she asked for a chair, she'd be asking for a table.

A room.

A house.

A country.

A name.

A story with meaning.

An afterlife.

She'd be asking for a God who heard and answered. Who wouldn't rage fire across the African and Australian plain. Who would show the world more clearly he was there.

Yes. Now the trucks were teepees moving on the hill. She could identify with Burlington and other names of migration. Tarps flopping like the loppy run of a young elephant. His penis nearly reaching the ground. Ribbons of clouds over the fields. The little white pebbles of the cows. It was like switching television channels.

Every time the man ahead of her got on his car phone he slowed down. Why couldn't he talk and drive at the same speed? She took the mantle of father who had been a driver and put it on her shoulders. Now she imagined her father as a pilot over the humps of air. Those mounds in space the mound builders left when they traveled to the beyond. Those humps in the air a plane passed over.

For a while she followed a man in a pickup with a sense of order. She felt the leaves. The shiny road. The precision of his driving.

While God was in his aloneness above the clouds, hoarding unanswered prayers on his lap, his wholeness sat on the road. The farm pond and fields. God of Lot who offered his daughters to the mob. Who made people full of flaws. Or let them get that way on their own. Who filled the earth with the autumn trees soaking in the light.

Sometimes a little elephant pulled though. She remembered his first wobbly reach to drink from his mother. The tears in her eyes. Her thought that her daughters and granddaughter and aunt would pull through. She would also. Because somewhere over the fields she traveled, there was a God of the highway. A God of the road.

Carleen felt as if she'd turned into the universe and was crisscrossing the stars. Yes, if there was one road left, she'd take it herself.

The Birds with the Breeze
of Their Wings

> *My father's name was* Crow that flies high with a
> yellow breast going on down to his tail feather.
> *The interpreter said,* just call him Yellowtail.
> *That's how he got on the roll.*
>
> ROBERT YELLOWTAIL
> Crow Reservation, Montana

He hears the voices of the machinery. The harvesters' snap on
their wheels. They parade the open plain. He sees the chaff
and dirt clods fall from them like spatters of rain. The trucks
piled high with clouds and Fig Wheeler's crop duster and the
birds all named Bunzo. Who roost in abandoned houses, the
ones without doors and window glass.

Then winter and the air abbreviated with sleet.

A Later Game of Marbles

> *Once the earth and sky were one. There was no*
> *room to stand. No light to see. Everyone crawled*
> *around in darkness. A flock of birds thought they*
> *could lift the sky. They flew up into the dark. The*
> *sky split and revealed the sun. That's why birds are*
> *first to greet the dawn.*
>
> from an aboriginal myth

[On a trip to Central Australia, I saw the Aboriginal dream-paintings, which tell stories of the land with a series of dots, something like an early stage of pointillism. I also wanted to tell a story with clumps of words like the mounds of spinifex grass over the landscape I saw from Ayers Rock, which are the genesis of the dots. Writing that way was like hearing someone trying to speak after a long silence. Or like hearing someone talk who was out of breath. I even tried numbering the paragraphs in a *paint-by-number* effect, but later removed them.]

The crows cawed. just before. dawn.

He heard them. he thought. at first light. but later he knew it was earlier. before he woke. when the dream-givers were. still shooting marbles. *click. click.* he heard them as he woke.

The dream-givers. came early. when he first entered. the dark sky of sleep. their faces swirled red and black. with flames. corkscrews. popeyes. Joseph coats. lutzes. oxbloods.

They walked. without sound. only their game made noise.

They had to get into his head. to keep his thoughts. on earth.

Otherwise. he could slip forever. away from darkness into true dark.

Maybe the crows. slit the dark. to let in the waking.

He knew the crows. spoke to him.

He tried to listen. past the hush of the dream-givers. who knew he was. awake now. a change in his breathing. or quick movement. that didn't belong to sleep.

He rubbed his head. and the sleep. from his eyes.

The dawn was blue. as the shirt pocket. where the denim hadn't faded.

He picked up. the shirt from the chair. got dressed.

The dream-givers were. surely gone. now they'd done their work. turning the darkness. inside out. spilling him to the floor. like chaff from a pocket. or pants-cuff. or marbles from a table.

The sun was. over the edge. of the cabin.

What kept him. here?

Though the crows. had done their work. he could still hear them. caw.

They were darkness. to the light. as the moon was. light to the dark.

His neck ached from sleep. his head felt heavy. damp as bacon.

He would go through the day. his heart. wrapped in baling wire.

He wanted to be. with the ancestors. he remembered his great-grandfather. rolling marbles in his hand. the gooseberries. marshmallow cores.

That's what drinking. did eventually. stopped the dreams. so he could cross. to the other world.

Maybe his dog would. be waiting for him. there. yes. dreams were. the animals of nature.

He drank from a bottle of. whiskey. ate a stale. piece of fry bread.

He remembered following. his grandma. to the chicken coop. the hens cackled. like a fire just lit. from kindling. or a game of marbles.

He remembered his grandma's. patched dress. her large shoes. their tongues all parched. dust on them. like something. he was supposed to remember. but kept getting away.

He felt the moon. half-light. half-dark. the moon was also light. for the dream-givers. playing *ringer*.

He thought he heard hens. cackling. no. that was the dream-giver. with orbs and shooters painted on his forehead.

Maybe the crows were. fragments of. blackness broken. because of light.

The earth was. his grandmother. unable to take care of him. anymore. because she was sick. now he followed her. not even knowing. how to turn. for the sun's warmth. on both sides.

It was the day. that was hard. someday he'd escape. the earth. its bright light. into dark.

Someday he'd sleep. and not return. he'd pass from. ordinary dark into. true dark that shut out the earth.

The dream-givers. could throw. as many dreams at him. as they wanted. they could hit his head. until it jumped like a sack-full of agates.

He wouldn't come back. no. he'd be gone. there's nothing they. nor the crows. nor anyone. could do.

More than ever. now. when he started. his old truck. he wanted the night. when the moon. followed the earth.

What bothered him? the wife. he'd not. been able to keep?

Even the animal. chose to leave. no. the dog. had been made to leave.

He remembered something. kicking. was it his leg. or what?

Sometimes. the crows yelped. like a hurt dog.

Maybe. the groaning was. from his own throat.

When he got to work. he'd be late. in trouble again. he didn't want. to think about it.

He remembered. climbing the hill. behind his grandpa's farm. the clumps. of birches between. the narrow fields. the creek that. dried in summer. the rocks. from the sweat lodge spoke to him.

Sometimes. in his stupor. he tried to turn to light. but too much. had happened.

Yet. there was something in him. that resisted. true darkness. something that sent. the dream-givers.

Maybe that was the nature. of the landscape. inside his head.

He had in himself. the struggle of light. dark.

Maybe he had to learn to face. both. but where did they. come from? was the Creator. a Trickster? sometimes. the crows seemed. to laugh.

Or was the Creator. a giving Spirit? who sent light. not the ordinary glare. men brought. into their lives. by their own efforts. and had to live with. no. but true light.

Did he have to choose between. the possibilities?

Would he always roll. like marbles spinning. changing places on the floor.

All right. then. it was light for the moment. he'd face. the Creator's light.

But. someday he'd be through. then he could. follow the ancestors.

He'd go back. to his grandpa's place. he'd hear him call him *peewee* again. he'd climb the hill. behind the sweat lodge.

Yes. he'd see. the clouds overhead.

It was only. a *click*. up there to the sky.

Crossing the Specific

[*Passing the James Range on the edge of Simpson Desert, South of Alice Springs, Hugh River, near Stewart's Well, on the way to Ayers and Olgas Rocks, Northern Territory, Central Australia, someone says*
    10,000 miles to Australia—
        you have to see sunset at Uluru, Ayers Rock]

Australia's upside down. Invert it. Reverse it. Look through from the other side. The shape of the continent is something like America without Florida. Nearly as large. But with emu. Kangaroo. Land cruisers crusted with red mud. Verandas under ghost gums in the outback.

Pruny hadn't wanted to leave America. She had an idea about being connected to the land. To leave one's land was a journey of death. She felt her existence was tied with the land. To depart from it she'd risk her connection. Yet she was with her companion on a trip.

At first she looked for the familiar. Cars driving the accustomed side of the road. Brands in the grocery. Constellations. Not the Southern Cross.

At Steffon Cottage in the Blue Mountains near Sydney. She bought some tomato/prune jam. *Forget comparisons to America. She would not look back,* she said. She also bought the jam because her name was Prunella. Where had her mother gotten that? Tom, her companion, still asked.

In a bookstore, Pruny bought a book of aboriginal stories to read on the tour bus to Alice Springs. *Only visitors buy these,* the woman said.

And they bin turnem round and shootem all.
All people, all, like bullock.
Old people bin here, this country.
All bullock, like bullock. Big mob we got it.
Oh, woman . . . kid . . . man.
Too much woman.
Too much . . .
Too much blackfeller.
All Warlpiri, you know, all Warlpiri.
Poor bugger.

LIKE BULLOCK, JIMMY JUNGARRAYI,
WARLPIRI, YUENDUMU,
from *Long Time, Olden Time, Aboriginal Accounts of Northern Territory History*, collected and edited by Peter and Jay Read, Institute for Aboriginal Development Publications, Sydney, 1991

There was a big rock. In the middle. Tom said he was going to climb. Just over a mile. Ayers Rock. It looked straight up. But there was a chain-link rail. Up the steepest part. Which came first. Pruny thought she'd follow Tom just a ways. She wasn't planning on climbing. She had her heavy shoulder purse she couldn't leave on the tour bus. But she was wearing her walking shoes.

All the climbers stopped every few feet to rest. Everyone panted for breath. Pruny gripped her thighs already. To quit. She had to take it slow. Some turned back. Panicked. As they felt the ascent against the side of bare rock. She could fall off the earth here.

Pruny knew why all the Japanese could live on a small island. At any given time. At least half traveled to other lands.

They had two hours. For the climb. And return. Then the tour bus left for the lodge after the morning climb.

The first time Pruny looked back. She understood the pointillism of the aboriginal dream-painting she'd bought in Alice Springs when they first arrived. *Two snakes came from the sky. To make nests. Moved on. Left waterholes in the desert.* She saw the spinifex. Round clumps of grass. That dotted the landscape. Just like the painting. She pointed them out to Tom. *See. And the roads look serpentine.*

She'd heard the aboriginals didn't climb the rock. She laughed to her companion. But how else could they know the way the land looked from the air? Maybe in dream-flight?

The end of the chain rope was a third of the way. The largest part of the trip was still ahead. Over the top of the rock. She must not have heard. But she hadn't thought she'd climb.

Go on. She told Tom.

Pruny rested while. Japanese tromped by. And by. Clicking pictures. Some older than Tom and Pruny. Talking in their language. Pointing out the height. Looking back. *Ahhhh!* Is all she understood.

Who cared if she reached reached the top? She was high enough. Didn't she speak her world into being? Wasn't she on an Australian walkabout? Wasn't she in alternate, post-modern realities? Well. Pruny claimed. This. The real top.

She looked down at the tour buses. The flat. Red land of central Australia. The Olgas. The neighboring rocks in the distance.

Uluru was made by two boys playing in the mud. Pruny liked that story.

Or it's where *Tjukuppa*, the spirit beings, took the form of ancestors, or first ones, and walked the earth speaking words that made the water holes and sand dunes, the acacias, the mulgas and eucalyptus, the clumps of spinifex or porcupine grass.

That was called dreamtime, and when the ancestors rested, their large heads became the *Kata Tjuta*, or the Olgas, *Uluru's* neighboring rocks.

Pruny even got to decide which version of the origin of *Uluru* to hear.

On top of the rock, she saw the ridges. Yes, she saw the rock was marked by the hands of the giant boys scooping sand, forming it into a huge loaf on the land. She saw where the mud had squeezed between their fingers before it hardened into rock. Yes, she knew it. The landscape had been left to boys playing at the shore.

Pruny decided to climb on. Over the red rock. Which was sandstone. Full of iron. Rusting, in other words.

People who had reached the top were now on their way back. Those who spoke English said. *There's a point across the top of the rock. There's a cairn there. Keep going.*

She had to look at her fear of not being able to do it. Of falling off. There was some thought. If she did this. She could do others. And if she stopped short. She would be mapping her way to fall short of her dreams.

Where did she get the ideas that drove her? What were her dreams before she shriveled and turned more prunish?

Ayers Rock was a loaf of bread. A large loaf. Sliced. She counted the slices. Across the top. Rock layers stood straight up. Nothing more than a lump of red bedrock pushed 1,100 feet in the air. By some ancient earthquake.

The top of the rock was a rolling terrain. Not just a rounded rock. But gulleyed. The sharp ridges were hardest to walk. There were white footprints to follow then. Like the white line down the middle of an old highway. A gentle roller coaster. Or a snake. Side-winding.

And there was Tom, her companion. Several gulleys ahead.

The cold wind whipped around her. Pruny tied a wool scarf on her head. She kept climbing. Sometimes on all fours. Her shoulder bag hitting her knee she brought forward to climb. She felt awkward. Sometimes she slipped a little. But her walking shoes finally took grip.

The wind pushed so hard at times she felt her heavy purse was all that held her down.

Would Jesus have done this? The thought seemed to come from nowhere. Yes. She decided. Ayers Rock reminded her of the Stations of the Cross. Their interrupted fragments. Joined this time by aboriginals. Kangaroo and emu.

Some of the steps:

(1) Waved by palm branches clumped as spinifix.

(2) Round up.

(3) Trial and error.

(4) *And they bin turnem round and shootem all.*
    All people, all, like bullock.
    Poor bugger.

(5) The crucifying.

(6) Farther from generalities.

(7) The resurrected.

(8) The risk of losing connection.

Pruny remembered the aboriginal belief. You walk the land into being. Or sing it. Maybe. The land not there until you say it was.

She spoke the cairn to her feet.

She wouldn't be able to do this. Possibly ever again. If she came back. She probably wouldn't climb. No. She wouldn't do this again until she flew in death. Higher than this pebble. You bet. She'd leave Ayers Rock far behind.

Finally. She was standing at the cairn. Over 1,000 feet in the air. She'd climbed it on her own. Wind battering her jacket.

The wool scarf vibrating on her head. Her companion surprised she was behind him.

Looking down at Australia from Ayers Rock. She felt like she'd reached a landing in the stairs. With only air around it. To take off from. Up there were the other high places she'd been. The Statue of Liberty's head. Long's Peak in Colorado. The barn loft on her grandfather's farm.

She looked at her watch. It had taken an hour and a half to reach the cairn on top where they rested a few minutes. And descended in thirty-five. Missing the bus.

The climb down seemed harder. She felt the descent in her knees. Her legs quivered. She tried once turning around to come down backward. It was too hard to see where she was going.

They asked for a ride back to the lodge with some girls touring Australia.

The next day. Tom and Pruny left from the airport to return to Sydney. Their legs sore. Every move. Pained. She felt she could hardly walk. On the plane, she looked back at the rock. Staying behind. Alone on the land. Until it disappeared from her window. The way she looked at something. She knew she'd never see again.

Maybe that was her dream. To have the voices of hardship put away in a book she carried in a shoulder purse. Just once. To be a tourist. To have several versions of a story.

She had journeyed across a rock. Someone said they had to see. Upside down. Without Florida. Out of reach.

That was her dream-flight. To see the land she spoke into being. To feel the way words fell back in the updraft. Some called the verge of stone.

In the Burrito

Layla lived in the *burrito*, as she called it, with her husband, Saldo. Deglazing the ham, refrying the potatoes. He wasn't really her husband. But he was her man and his children were her stepchildren.

At first she'd had a husband. Not the father of her children. But her husband had married her and been a father to her children. They'd even had a child, who lived with him now. But what thought had he had in his head? She finally left from boredom in the fireless marriage.

Her father had made sure she had what she wanted. He'd provided. When she left her husband, she moved in with her father. After her mother died.

Layla'd never married the father of her children. He was the father of most of them anyway. He wasn't the man for her. He kept hanging around, yes. A hang-around-the-fort. As long as it was convenient. She wasn't being fair. Just angry.

Then he stopped coming around.

At first it didn't hurt.

But after a while, Layla climbed the walls.

She moved in with her father again. By then he had another wife, who let her know the house was crowded.

Then she lived with a girlfriend. But their kids fought. So did they.

Then she'd had relationships. But they never worked.

Now she lived with Saldo in a low bungalow with blue print curtains and a front-porch roof like a frown.

How did she get there? One wrong turn after another.

Then there was a freak snow.

She saw the old woman across the street crawling on her hands and knees in her yard. Her old hound dog baying. Had she fallen? Her blue dress, boots, her wool jacket, a scarf around her head. The old woman looked confused. Quickly, Layla threw a blanket over her shoulders, ran out and saved her.

Their picture was in the paper. The old woman and the hound dog and Layla and Saldo and her children and stepchildren and her former husband, who was a firefighter.

After their picture was in the paper, the ardor returned.

Layla cooked that Mexican sausage, *chorizo con huevos*, wrapped with beans and chilis in a flour tortilla.

Molé.

She remembered grade-school fevers. High-school sunburns. The smell of wildfire burning in the field, sparked from lightning. She remembered the comets. The book burnings.

The salsa.

The traffic of boyfriends and lovers, husbands and former husbands, children and stepchildren, girlfriends and their children, mothers and stepmothers.

She'd wanted a simple life. Where had the clutter come from? Their blankets folded over them. All their lives inside.

You Know Those People Don't Talk

The real me, the one nobody sees, is an old Indian woman. My grandmother who died when I was young. She didn't have time to tell me who I was. What my name would be. What animal would be mine to change into when we changed to animals at night.

When my daddy got out of the army, he said he was going to marry the first girl he saw when he got off the bus in Arkansas. The first girl was my mamma.

They got married, but he was on the bus again before I was born.

Mamma had an old dog. She said Daddy told him to watch us when he left. But the dog was killed before I was born. Hit by a pickup.

When I was born I had this mark on my forehead. You can see it if the light is right.

That's the way they were. Mamma weeding a few turnips in the garden. Grandma on the porch twisting tobacco, saying nothing, looking at me. The dog run over. The mark on my head. As if the two were connected.

Mamma said sometimes she could see him on the road at night.

Conjurers. Those women along the road. They knew when someone was coming. They could lift anyone's ear and hear [i:gawe':sdi] the stories inside.

When grandma died my mother didn't say anything. She could sit in the house at night and not move. They talked, you know, without saying anything.

My mother married again.

Later I had a brother.

He heard the story of the dog. *Roofer*, he called me. *Pal.*

If a dog would howl, they'd look at me.

I liked to go to Sunday school. The foil attendance stars with glue on the back side were like the stars that talked at night.

Sometimes in the church stories I got to be the leper. Sometimes we raised grandma from the dead with her licorice hair. I don't think she liked it. She never said anything. But it was her face that made me think that.

Oh I didn't believe in afterlife, the way they talk about it in Sunday school. Sitting up there in rows behaving yourself all the time.

No.

I could hear those women along the road humming like fire bees. The [*das' das' das'*] of the sumac logs in the fire. I could hear their sweet fire.

But having a dress now of the finest light, I saw grandma return to the after-land. She wasn't anything you could touch with your fingers. She was more like breath, or fog, or sound, as if hearing the old land.

All those stories in her head.

Eatin a raccoon with the little people.

[yv:wi tsu:n(a)sdi':i (people/small, they)]

Clearing the bones from the table.

Putting them in a barrel near the fire.

After a while, you could take the lid off

and the raccoon would climb out

and run back to the woods.

Sometimes when I'm not thinking about it, I can almost remember when I was young and they were in the other room. The little feet of the raccoon shucking the floor.

Grandma was tall and awkward. She was like clothes when they were stiff with starch. On a winter evening when she took them off the rope in the yard, a dress would stretch its arms across the bed, a slip would turn like an oar.

She was a shelf of a woman with a few crude bowls, some roots and herbs, and twists of tobacco. Maybe a woodpecker somewhere.

She always had *[i:gawe':sdi]*, an old thought-song on her mind. Not said out loud. But you could hear it. Over and over you could hear.

Sometimes I'd wear girl-clothes. They slowed me down. I'd be out with the stars and a skirt would not let me step.

What does daddy look like? I'd ask. Sometimes I think I see him on the road. We'd talk about rabbit hunting. Sometimes I hear their old language. If only I could understand.

My mother's gone now too.

I haven't told my children about any of them. What would they want to know for?

We fish Tenkiller now. My husband and I. The lake lapping at the boat.

Out on the water I can hear a dog bark from anywhere. Sometimes I think of the little people. I feel the lake rise right up there under the sky.

My husband can fish all day. He tells the children, *she sits in the boat and don't say nothing. You know those people don't talk.*

My brother's got a place over near Viola. I call his wife now and then.

Sometimes out on the lake, I can put my hand up there and feel their faces. Mother and Grandma. Even Dad. They're changing shape, transmuting into one form after another, rolling all over the sky.

Sometimes their thoughts pass like a motorboat.

Then Grandma puts her fingers through my arm. I think she feels the mark like a shallow place in my forehead.

Yes, they're with me. Sometimes even my husband now too.

You know it first in your toes, then up through your knees, your stomach, your neck, all the way up to the brain, which is the lake of the head.

You know I think I was a badger in the night. I felt the bones of a small animal in my teeth. Once I changed into a mole. The sharp smell of soil zinged my nose. I found dirt under my fingernails in the morning. I could lift my hands and see the stars.

Sometimes I hear Grandma try to tell me who I am. About the time I turn into Sonic in my Easter-egg blue Comet, I know she's in the backseat smacking beets and blackjack gum.

I wave to Cleora and Ernesta in a hairnet, parked at the curb, drinking their custom Cokes, venetian blinds in their back window, and peel into the street again over the black, spinning tires of the moons.

Jupter

She sits on the porch. Night jumping her lap. When she looks she can see the long haul. It was Jupter, the horse, running ahead. He took off in a buzz. She could say *odeeee* and he'd run faster. She could follow him through the cornstalks not knowing what was ahead. A ditch beside the road. A gulley that would send her spinning. That would stop her like a whack. *Always zero*, she says, *that's what space is*. The trees *zoaming* their light.

A neighbor spatters the stars with his gun. She thinks it's him. The one who shoots the stars. Someone has to. They're coming close taking the dark they need. The stars're birds now without their wings.

Those stars, if they ever get near air with gravity in it, they'll fall faster than history.

The neighbor sits in the hammock rocking himself. She knows it as she passes.

It's the horse with mane braided like sweet grass that tells her. With moons on his head. With a tail raining across the hills. It's Jupter snorting out there. Must be something in his way. A jet stream. A jet. He jumps them like hurdles. If he doesn't get by them, their after drag pulls him out of his way. He's a sparkler in the day sky. A bat at night. He's humming round the earth. *Don't be a luggard*, he says, *don't be that little spray of bat fat*.

Odelet sprays the zinnias in her flower bed when she gets back. Shoots them full of water from the spigot in the dark. She hears the water spirits jumping the grass. The blue trees. Magenta leaves. The house all full of hoofprints if she *don't* shut the door.

The Man Whose Voice Was in Travel

Cherry bomb, they called her.

Cherry breath.

A cherry is small and round and has a stem. Something like a match. The one she struck when she lit her first cigarette.

Cherry pit, they called her.

Cherry bone.

An ear growling with hunger for stories.

Cherry rode her bicycle down the road. It was a long trip between the winding trees. Sometimes a man on his bicycle passed. Her bike something like riding the moon. Her family the stars that seemed to change places each time she came back.

Her name was Cherry so she could remember the street she lived on. That was long ago. When Cherry lived in Searcy. Now she lived in Bee Branch, Arkansas. In a small house by the Full Gospel Church.

Cherry made dolls from scraps in the rag drawer. She tied string around their wrists to make hands. She sewed red beads on their faces. You know the way animal eyes look in the headlights when the truck turns in the drive or when an angel looks from a dark room when you turn on the hall light?

Maybe Cherry made the dolls because she thought they'd tell her stories. She tied them on the basket on her bicycle. She rode them down the road. She stuck sticks in their mouths for cigarettes.

A man plowed with angels he named like mules, the dolls said. The angels had jawbreaker eyes and loud lips when they kissed. Their teeth jelled in their heads. The angels laughed and sneezed in their harnesses. Dowsed with meadow ragweed you know this time of year.

Cherry saw the earth break into the soil of the universe where she rode her bike when the dolls talked. Over her the sky was like a long corridor where angels stepped when they finished their plowing.

Out there the moon romped in its yard. The shape-changer moon. It was always the same, Cherry knew, but from her perspective, the moon could look different on different nights.

The Full Gospel Church ruled these fields between the hills. The minister was out in them. Praying the crops out of the stingy ground. Praying the weeds and varmits back into their holes.

Cherry head, they called her.

Cherry ass.

Cherry's father was a do-all for the church. Leaf-work in the gutters. Grass-work in the cemetery. But sometimes he'd go off to the far parts of Arkansas. Ozone on Highway 21. Snowball on 74. Sometimes he'd tell the Middle Fork of the Little Red River to part. Then he'd walk to Evening Shade at the junction of 58 and 167. Or Beverage Town on 95. When the water parted for him, yes, like the sky.

Then the Full Gospel Church would pray him back.

Cherry's dolls had the pollen-voice of bees. Sometimes she could hear them from their little houses behind the neighbor's yard. Something in their buzz reminded her of heaven. Sometimes when God spoke she could hear the click of his eyelashes he just glued on so he could blink.

Cherry's dolls told her stories about Jesus. The savior of their elbows. The washer of their feet with blood. They told her the angels wouldn't bite when she crossed the pasture. She could withstand an army. She could go without eating and be fed. She could wink.

The dolls thought they could do anything with their stories.

They said Jesus came to find Cherry because she was from a family of cherry-tree choppers. Separated from honesty. Out of step.

The dolls were supposed to tell Cherry stories she wanted them to tell. What did they know anyway? And how could they talk without a heart?

The minister sneezed in church.

Isaiah 43:18 Remember not the former things, neither consider the things of old.

19 Behold, I will do a new thing; now it shall spring forth; shall ye not know it?

After the sermon, Cherry smoked behind the church as if it were a fireworks stand on the hill. She tromped down the furrows after the angels plowed. She stole a jawbreaker from the jar at Smith's. Yes, she stole an angel's eye.

Cherry could follow her father if it wasn't for the dolls talking Jesus. Spuzzed between the light and dark just like that light bulb behind the church with its electric heart.

But Jesus traveled.

Cherry read the Bible on the altar of the church while her father mowed. She read the parts about Jesus in red words. Cherry red.

Jesus had traveled from Bethlehem. Egypt. Nazareth in Galilee. The wilderness. Jerusalem. Capernaum. The desert. Gerasenes. Tyre. Sidon in the region of Decapopolis and Dalmanutha. He migrated through wheat fields. Across mountains. To villages of Chorazin. Bethsaida. Mazaden. Caeserea. Back to Capernaum. The regions of Judea beyond the Jordan. Jericho. Bethphage and Bethany again. Back to Jerusalem. The Mount of Olives. Golgotha. The road to Galilee. Hell. Heaven.

Geezo.

Cherry snapped a match and lit another *ret*. Hell was living with herself doing only what she wanted. Let the dolls tell that story.

She nailed her dolls' outstretched arms to the crossrails of the fence beside the church when her father left. Crucified them because they told stories of Jesus. She kept nailing them and nailing them because they talked about Jesus. Pounding and pounding.

Then their voices came, not from their mouths, which were stretched opened in a large O, but from everywhere. The beehouses. Clumps of trees. From behind the shed behind the church. From Jesus who was a dancer at the cherry-tree chopper's ball.

They could talk about her father. They could call her names. When their heads nodded during sermons she would be awake with stories. They could say, *Cherry picker, Cherry eye,* when she passed. Jesus was like her. Stuffed with cherry blood.

(clumpt) Jesus spoke (clumpt) because he was old now. Those were his dentures, Cherry thought.

Yes, that's what the minister said the people were supposed to do. Praise God. It was their job on earth. It's what they did in Bee Branch, Arkansas, at the Full Gospel Church. There were other chores. Giving an ear to the Lord so they'd know his will.

Cherry took her dolls off the fence where she'd crucified them. She took a string and formed a coil like an ear and sewed it on her dolls. Maybe the ears weren't big enough and she sewed on more ears. There were ears all over her dolls. At night they could hear out into the sky. They could hear Jesus when he turned in bed at night. They could hear him when he got up in the morning. Maybe he took the bus with her father to the far parts of Arkansas. Maybe he would be at the bus stop telling her father not to go. What made a man want to travel?

Sometimes now she was sure she heard Jesus. He talked to her as though they were friends. He tromped down the fields after the angels had plowed them. He wanted Cherry to follow him into the darkness of the human heart. That's where the light switch of Jesus was. Cherry knew the darkness feared the light. She felt it shrink during Bible lessons. Sometimes the darkness inside her was only an upturned bug with its legs kicking the air.

But Jesus came to tear up the old ways. To let the new people, the Gentiles, and even the Indians, into his kingdom because the Jews wouldn't come. Jesus was at the cherry-tree chopper's ball and the Jews said, *hey I'm not coming because you're not the son of God you don't look like a king.* But Jesus says he was the son and he invites us to his house to get their place. If we believe. Yo. We have to call the name of Jesus. On his bicycle he rides past the houses to see what we're doing like this man who rides his bike. Cherry thought he might be Jesus. He had a basket on the handlebars like hers. He'd stop and pick up stuff. His house was probably full of junk. Cherry didn't speak to him. He didn't seem to see her. Yes. He was Jesus. Riding his bike to find out who he could collect. Cherry kept riding past him. She tied her dolls to the basket on her bike so they wouldn't fall out. Her dolls with all their ears. The darkness wouldn't get her. No. If she belonged to Jesus who rode his bike around Arkansas though he looked like the ragman to Cherry.

Do you want to see heaven do you want to be the cherry on the cake of the human heart? The minister's voice touched her ear on Sunday. Yes. He touched her with his voice. Flipped the light switch. Killed the darkness. She felt peeled back like thick branches of the scrub oaks along the road. He'd give her a cherry heart. Yes. She'd take Jesus as her savior.

At the altar the minister called her a secret name. *Cherith.* The brook where God fed Elijah. Yes, he just sent the ravens with some bread. Later Cherry looked in the Bible. But the brook dried up. But it filled again with rain. That was it. This shape-changer earth. Just like the moon. This way one minute another the next. Get used to it.

Yes. The bicycle man looked like a ragpicker but Cherry knew he was Jesus himself. Who rode his broken-down bicycle one minute, and his angels the next. Who was the same always, but from her viewpoint depending on what day it was, looked thin as the ragman one day and fat as the moon the next.

That's what the bee-buzz was about. The sneezing voices. All the noise of heaven and earth.

Cherry could follow her father and that traveling-man Jesus. Mover and maker. She could do anything with her faith. In the new bee box of her head. Jesus would be stronger than her will to do only what she'd wanted. She would be part of the cherry juiced. The cherry fed.

Sumac

A girl / she was. / Then / the girl / went in search of a vision.
/ *Ten days / I am going / and / if not/ I return / you / will think /
already / something / kills her.* / But / here / her friend / very
dear. / Then / she went / and / he followed her. / With an
arrow / he shot her. / Not / anywhere / could he put / the
arrow. / He would hide it / and / go away / and / always /
he would see it. / There / he said / *Confound it! / Where shall I
put it?* / When / then over that way / he shot it / the arrow
stuck amid / sumac. / And / not / anywhere / he saw it. /
Now / then / he went home / and / there / he would weep /
the girl. / And saying to himself *How could it be of me / they will
suspect me / that he / killed her.* / Thus / he sang / just / he is
weeping. / And / he is / younger brother / just / he plays /

54

spearing targets / with arrows / and he sings / he too / *my* /
girl / *my girl.* / And / his mother / said to him / *What is that* /
thus / *you keep saying?* / *Just* / *my elder brother* / *I often hear he*
sings / *and* / *just I am imitating him.* / His mother / here / said
to him / the father / *Now probably it is that* / *he killed her.* /
Because / now / ten / days / and the girl's mother / wept / and
opens wide her mouth / looks / toward the mountain / that
which way / hers went / daughter. / (It was the boy / when /
he killed her / the girl's hair / he cut hers off / and / that / he
holds while / he grieves.) / Then / she wept / the old woman
/ like / this / she open wide her mouth / she weeps. / A fly
precisely / true / her mouth / it flew into / and / at once /
she bit it / the fly / burst open / thereupon / the fly / fetid /
and / she said to herself / the old woman / *Already it is that*
mine / *dead* / *is* / *child.* / Then / they searched for her / the girl
/ because / now / the old woman / all of them / said to them
/ *Dead* / *she is.* / And / they went / to the mountains / looking
for her. / Then / there / they found her. / It was that / even /
he had buried her / but / they found her / and they saw /
that / shot she is / and / they searched for that / with which
/ he had shot her. / Absolutely / absent / arrow / anywhere.
/ All about / they searched / not ever / the arrow they found.
/ Here / they took home / the body / and / there / they
buried her / and not ever / they found / who killed her /
because / not arrow they found his. / But from / there / it
became / sumac / red / the girl's / blood.

Spikes

She had spikes of light on her head. If you touched them you would bleed. You had to look at them from a distance. If you got close, you'd get hurt.

Sometimes the spikes came from her neck and chest. Thorns of light.

Yet they worshipped her in that church. She must listen to their jabbering. Maybe she has wings like helicopter blades that come from her head. But she doesn't pray to Jesus. She hides their true eyes from the light that is Jesus. She doesn't access the other.

> John 12:49   For I have not spoken of myself, but the Father, who sent me.

What's she doing at the window like she's the authority? You think she's throwing a spike of her light.

You notice first a limp in your hip. It hurts to walk. If you sit for a while it's hard to get up and walk with your plate and cup to wash and dry them with your little towel on its nob.

You will not think of it. You will not pray to her though they tell you she will help. You see she sucks the light into herself and she's supposed to be only a sidecar.

It's Jesus who died for your sins. Didn't he tell her to stand aside? He was serving wine or something. He told her to stay out of the way and not tell him what to do.

The thorns of light poke from her head. When you sleep she comes through the door. You feel her slash, yet she is not the full light. When you wake, you tell her she is not drooling over you.

You tell her to go outside. You tell her Jesus gave her to one of his disciples when he died on the cross. John or Simon Peter or one of them.

She stands on the porch like a prickly bush.

Somehow with her thorns she opens the door.

She's not giving them the whole story. She puts them in her frame of reference. Disconnects them from their source.

In your little bedroom, you feel like a field of sheep waking. You need a shepherd.

You tell Jesus you think it's one of her thorns in your hip. You feel him rustling your bones to find it.

When she comes to the window you say there's a church with a statue of her inside. A virgin statue with an arrow in her heart. If she could get the arrow to bleed, she'd have even more people praying to her. I see her from the corner of my eye looking down the road thinking if she should go there.

In your isolation and roughness, in your hurt you need Jesus. Not his mother speaking to him for you. You can speak to him yourself. You can say to her, *lady, buzz off.*

Yet you have to have respect. She's felt death and some disappointment. She was a mother. Maybe that's why she takes revenge. She wants to do what they did to her son. You hardly know what she wants.

But you know what she's doing, in part, anyway. That shifty little firefly. She's a shortener of meaning. A caller of the lies.

The Great House

. . . whistling with drafts, clattering with hail.
POPOL VUH, PART THREE

She sat at the table with her earmuffs on.

The Black Jack dealer dealt her cards.

9.

2.

Hit me.

3.

Hit me.

8.

Busted.

5.

6.

Hit me.

4.

Hit me.

Jack.

Busted.

Would you take your earmuffs off?

Is there a law?

Take them off.

She stuffed them in her pocket.

Now she was going to toss her coins into the casino machines and they would spill for her.

Thop.

Thop.

Thop.

Already she could hear them drop.

There was something about the machines with their arms raised that reminded her at first of baseball players with their bats.

Yes. She was going to pitch her coins.

They were Umpires. Bearers. Begetters. Makers. Night keepers. Sovereign plumed serpent in the old Mayan ball games.

Mix masters.

One dealer.

Two dealer.

She was high on the game. There was a timelessness in gambling. Yet once in a while, she felt the now of it. She knew losers in the old court-ball games lost their heads. Even though she played casino machines instead of ball games, she still played for her life. The plumed serpent had its tongue in her throat. She could pet its wings.

She felt a chill and put on her earmuffs again.

The machine was not letting go. How could it do that? She heard the jingling voices of other machines. She heard something beyond that.

She could hear an old language if she wore her earmuffs. But she couldn't understand. What was it? An ancient market-place? A stone pounding metal? She jerked the handle over and over. The Guardian of the Temple came and said for her not to do that.

At least he didn't make her take off her earmuffs.

Inside the muffled sound was something far away and long ago.

Where was she?

The numbers owned her now.

Didn't she? Wasn't she always on the edge?

Now her fingers were like piano keys. She was playing the machines. She heard the music of the toy pianos.

She was a girl eating flowers with her friend. Pimpernels?— Something ingenious at six. Anything but the hunger she remembered. The empty house. A bare floor. Someone crying.

For a moment she was gone from the casino because she remembered, but soon she was back.

The sacrifice of flowers. Yes, but now she was the sacrifice.

Look at the flock of machines. They were a brood of snakes.

She could beat them. The magic would come back. If she just kept playing.

Who could she borrow from? What could she sell? Her landlady would be waiting. Even if it were late at night. She could stay at the shelter again. But not for long. Every place turned her out. Every place told her to move on. The nothingness closed in on her. There was nowhere to go.

One Pawn.

Two Pawn.

She was winging now over the casino. She heard the flight of machines. A covey of wild birds. Maker. Begetter. Over them, the plumed serpent, *Quetzalcoatl*, breathing on her. She went into other territories on his wings. The boundaries eased. The continent combined. She could hear the coins. The neon constellations of the machines. The casino was the cartoon of the cosmos.

Let the circuit breakers shut down. Turn them all into dark. Electricity was the God now. Let him withhold his light.

She was going nowhere.

Honeytail, you little gambling addict. You horsetail flyer, you one-arm wombat.

She knew the casino hovered above the land.

Twelve searchlights in a circle shined from the roof, intersected high in the air, then opened to the sky. Something like a giant hourglass of lights. Or two teepees meeting at their smoke holes, one sitting on the casino, the other reaching upside-down into the sky. Cold rain falling in the light like a neon marquee.

The whole dark night moved with the searchlights as if they were trails on which the buffalo returned.

Casino machines.

Black Jack.

Poker.

Keno.

Keno.

Poker.

Black Jack.

Casino machines.

She was in a *hizzup*.

Haywire.

Spin til you win.

Ball2on bars.

July 4.

Red white & blue.

Slam dunk.

1 home run.

Wild che2ry.

Earthcake.

Hu2ricane.

She could see numbers in the letters before her eyes.

The machines sounded their voices. Something like a toy piano. Something like roosters. Sometimes like voices from an old ball game. Or horns and traffic noise. That was the new story mixed with the old. The *thop thop* of the coins. How could they not spill?

Other times the machines sounded something like the voice of a flower beheaded.

Something like the screams of the pimpernel as it was eaten.

For a moment she was in the past again. It was her own history rolling across the far field.

Yes, in the casino she was on the slide.

That's what she liked about the machines though she hardly realized it. As she began to lose she got a rush. She had to get in gear. She had to find the momentum as she pulled the handle and saw the flash of cherries before her eyes.

Indian gaming. Reservation gambling. The old ball games came back. Sometimes the coins fell out.

Thop.

Thop.

She kissed them. Put them in the slot again. Swinging the handle of the baseball bat. Playing at the tables.

They stood around watching her. She was in a haze of dust from the ball field. The crowd roared. This was a game to the death.

She could see the severed heads in the casino.

Yes, it was the place of the ball-game sacrifice. But something more was going on. Something of which the casino was only a part. It was the nothingness she felt which swallowed her.

Umpires of the Bat handlers.
Bearers of the Bats.
Begetters of the Ball courts.
Makers of the Grandstands.
Night keepers of the coins.
Disappearing.

They were coming to remove her head. Before she saw too much.

But if they killed her she'd be a flower in the sky. Or a skull somewhere on the shelf like the moon above the Great House of the Casino.

Decapitated. With no place for her earmuffs.

No, the moon was an earmuff on the ear of the hollow universe.

Rattling House.

Cold House.

Great House full of drafts.

Continuous buzzing and humming.

Something was happening. She felt the fangs of the plumed serpent in her neck. It hardly hurt. She didn't know anything could be so easy.

Now the terror was over.

Something called her away. She could see through the roof. The searchlights above the casino were a shiny, twelve-lane road.

Yes, casino traffic was a new parade.

She waved to the spectators who waited for her along the road. Her hand moving. You know the way snow on a highway snakes.

They were all headless and they were calling her away.

She'd just put a few more coins in the machines and then she'd be done.

The Bird Who Reached Heaven

When Satan said, *jump*, Pastor Buddy Bob Bill didn't move. The congregation in his church, *In the Twinking of an Eye* (with an eyeball painted on the side of the white frame church), sat forward on their pews. They'd seen Buddy Bob wrestle at the altar. They didn't doubt Satan and his demons were there.

Sometimes the demons ran around the church at night. Sometimes they superimposed themselves on others. You could see a neighbor with a demon on his face. Sometimes Buddy Bob's wife, Vemoth, in her demon dress, would move from the back of the church to the front to show the people how a demon could stand right behind them and they'd hardly know it. Except Vemoth wore shoes that groaned when she walked. They always knew where she was. That's what caused the trouble. Buddy Bob preached. Not knowing the enemy.

And they warred against the Midianites, as the Lord commanded Moses, and they slew all the males . . . And they burned all their cities . . . And Moses said to them, Have ye saved the women alive? Behold, these caused the children of Israel to commit trespass against the Lord . . . Now therefore kill every male among the little ones, and kill every woman that hath known man by lying with him. (Numbers 31: 7, 10, 15–17.) Now tell me God doesn't mean business. Buddy Bob preached.

Tell me we're not supposed to know holiness and desperation. Pastor Buddy Bob Bill held the people spellbound. When Satan says, *jump*, we hear him and we jump. Those demons, those *polly-lops*, are in our heart because of him.

Pastor Buddy Bob Billy.

Pastor Brother Buddy Bob Billy Bub.

He was a matchstick to the tinder pile. He could talk to the hill folks. He could dance their backwood language. He could sit on their porch made with greenwood posts which spilt when they dried and caused the porch roofs to sway.

Brother Buddy Bob Billy was going to zap them. He was going to remove their demons. Keep their feet from jumping. Render Satan powerless before them. Transform them into the kingdom of light. Didn't they all know they were on earth to get destined to heaven? Jesus was the sanctifier. The water in the well. The drop the bucket made to get where it was going. Yes. Your heavenly life began *rite har on urth*. That's what the zooming was about.

The people sat looking at him. Sometimes they were a small congregation. A few farmers and their wives and children. A few old ladies. Sometimes others came and stayed for a while, but they left.

Often the mural Vemoth painted across the back of the church pulled in Buddy Bob's eyes more than his congregation. He could see it every time he looked up from the pulpit.

Vemoth had to keep painting. Even if it meant another eyeball on the church. She had to keep seeing new things. She had her own vision. Buddy Bob had to remember that. Though he tried to keep her from painting. It was the same as having her feet jumping all over the place.

She'd been one of the *Beebombers* when she went to Arkansas State. But that was over twenty years ago. Sometimes people remembered.

She'd studied the art of Frida Kahlo, that Mexican painter. *Feet why do I want them if I have wings to fly. Pies para que lost quiero, si tengo alas pa'volar.*

Sometimes Spanish would come from her mouth. *Diego mi amor. No se olvide que cabes el fresco nos juntaremos ya hara siempre* . . . Something like that.

She called her pictures, *Itzcuintli with Me. They Ask for Stones and Are Given Bread. Translation Mobile (a car with wings). True Hope and Desperation. Demon Love. Still Life with God. Self Portrait with Cropped Hair. Self Portrait with Demon Shoes.*

There's a lot of self portraits, Buddy Bob remarked. He warned her against self-seeking. Yes, but Vemoth was on the stage of her true station. Nothing would stop her. *Deportation,* she called a picture of the translation, when Christ's believers would leave this earth before the last *turrible* war called, Armageddon. Later, she changed the name to *Desportation,* because she loved the way Buddy Bob spelled.

Buddy Bob always glanced at Vemoth as he preached. How could she see a red sky and blue grass? How could she see a landscape all her own?

Sometimes he removed one too many demons. Then Vemoth was dull. Where was her *spuz?* She needed to *helt her haid to the urth to hear the old voices. Get out thar, Vemoth,* he commanded. *Or sid in har and hear the gospel.*

But later, she'd kick up and he'd put the squeezer on her again.

Sometimes she lashed back.

Haven't you ever thought Jesus might wrestle you to the floor, Buddy Bob, and knock some tolerance into you? Wasn't Christ a rebel? If Buddy Bob looked to Jesus, Vemoth looked to Frida Kahlo. What was the difference?

She continued painting and he frumped to his study.

Lord you can't mean it. Pastor Brother Buddy Bob saw her painting one morning. He parlayed into prayer as he watched her. A bird nearly large as the church in her mural? Standing there with its bare breast to the vestible? Standing there with its black demon eyes?

But that afternoon as Vemoth painted, Brother Buddy Bob Bill thought he saw his Savior. His rarefied light. The lamb-light always on behind the pulpit. He thought he saw Christ as a giant, yellow-breasted something. A finch (?) who could reach heaven. *And the meek shall inherit the blessings of the earth. And the meek shall inherit.*

Pastor Buddy Bob Bill prayed no one in *In the Twinking* would comment on Vemoth's painting. He heard her talk to her brush while she worked. *The barn lantern of his breast,* he heard her say. Vemoth told the bird in her painting the story of the loaves and the fish. Everything was relative. She had also painted a mural in the town cafe. More of her blue hogs. More of her delights. People stood there looking at it.

Even the demons must have looked.

On Sunday, Vemoth put away her paints. She ran through the church. Finding whom she could inhabit. Whom she could assist Brother Pastor Buddy Bob Billy Bub instill with the fear of demons and therefore the fear of God who was the only one who could drive the demons out. Yes Buddy Bob Bill *was only an instrument, congregation, not the force itself.*

We were mere *instrumentations* in his hands.

The high and holy one who inhabits the space between our lives.

We are high and lifted up. The choir hummed at the high intervals in Buddy Bob's sermon.

The wicked are like the tossing sea that cannot keep still.

Let's sit still and see who can be the stillest. Oh holy stillness the great stillness is your house. Yes, congregation, thank him for his blessings. Ask him for the strength to live. Seek wisdom so you'll know the voice of the demons so you can say, NO, THANK YOU, Satan, I'M NOT JUMPING.

Otherwise your boundaries are solid. The evil ground doesn't diminish.

While he spoke, someone moved and Buddy Bob saw him.

Pastor Brother Buddy Bob Billy turned to Vemoth in her demon dress. Wasn't she lovely? Brother Buddy Bob Billy swooned in the pulpit. Lust for his wife in her demon dress overcame him. He forgot what he was supposed to do.

Buddy Bob sweated as if he was chopping wood. A plump woman had to bring him a glass of water.

Pastor Buddy Bob sat dazed in the town cafe that Sunday after his sermon. He still wiped his sweat when he looked at her. *We fight the battle of faith*, he was fond of saying. *Look at that dog in the doorway. His nose twitching in the boxing ring of sleep.*

Vemoth drew the square-dancing stools on the back of her place mat. The knotty pine paneling. The wood varnish. The glass-plate window flashing cars turning from the curb as Buddy Bob spoke. The scene was pre-*Armageddonian* with DOOM in the background.

Though the fry cook's impatience was on the menu, Vemoth saw him now through the serving window where the food sat.

Vemoth borrowed Bubby Bob's place mat. She drew the checked tablecloths, the homemade *seasonals* weathering the small-town Arkansas, and all the talk a highway patrolman could muster.

Clinking silverware to looney tunes. Buddy Bob's eye still on her. She's a dear one. The dear new age. Godless as a group of hogs. Now the jukebox turned records faster than the fry cook's spatula. The blue-platespecial's going fast. The posters waffled on the wall when someone came in. At the door, the dog naps.

Yes, it's the *planetation* of a new orbit when you're in Christ when you're saved by the blood. Buddy loved his run-on sentences like Vemoth loved her demon paint.

Her great-great-grandparents had walked the Removal to Arkansas. Her people were backwood Cherokees who tried to blend. They went to church now and lived like hill folks. Building their porches with green wood. Hoping their porch roofs would sway. Stammering in the church in tongues.

Vemoth was getting ideas for another demon dress. He saw her drawing on another napkin. She ripped a dress almost everytime she wore it. Buddy Bob heard her turning the pages of her mind. It made him think of his next sermon.

There was the darkness. We all had it in our heart. Evil darkness that said, *I will.* Yes, that was the culprit. The voice of self-determination. It listened to itself until it heard nothing else. The *darkness* grew to *Darkness* to *DARKNESS* there was no stopping it there was no stop gate. Except the cross. We had to believe that. Evil was something in the heart. A self-centeredness that grew like kudzoo over Arkansas. Unchecked it could go on. And on. It was a matter of degrees. It was an attitude of the heart like yeast that could raise the whole lump. We had it in the ovens of Germany. Satan trying to get God to close down the century before it was time. To come back and rip the cord from the earth. Turn it off. Leave it stranded in space. Look at them other planets. Wooh! Who'd want to be like them? Cold and liverless or inferno hot. Unlivable. *Gizo.* It was all a matter of our *situational* to God. The farther away we got the more we were filled with demons. The higher our feet jumped for Satan. Just look at Northern Ireland. Africa. South America. Bosnia *Hertz-no-ginea,* Buddy Bob tried to say the name. The Holy Lands. Is there a place without darkness? No.

Brother Buddy Bob held his hand over his mouth. He was in the cafe getting ready to give another rip-tooting Sunday sermon. The fry cook would throw his spatula at him. If Buddy Bob let it all out he'd have trouble retrieving it next

Sunday. Still a week away. Sermons were like demons running loose if you let them. He held his mouth shut.

But the following Sunday the rest of the sermon was there. He opened his mouth again and there it was. We could grow evil as Hitler who killed folks in ovens, starved them to death. Brother Buddy Bob Bill felt a bitter intake of breath as he stood in his pulpit. He was getting to the heart. We're not dealing with ideas here. Evil has a smell. It has shape!

It was here that Vemoth ran from the back of the church. What made her to do that? Buddy Bob Bill turned from his sermon. He wasn't ready for her yet. But she bowed her arms to the floor. Lifted them to the ceiling. Up and down the aisle she undulated.

Not yet, Vemoth, I'm not to the demon part yet.

But she had her own phone. She was on her own flight. *Whad you doing? Come forth in the name of Jesus.* Vemoth stiffened as if hit by a bolt. She realized she'd been daydreaming at the back of the church and stunned now, she fell as if cleared of a demon herself. It whizzed around the room looking for a hog. It grunted and roared in her imagination. The congregation ducked, shooing it off. Buddy Bob commanded it to leave and it must have parted. There was a tinny sound trampling off the roof. Vemoth rose and walked up the aisle to the vestibule. Buddy Bob Bill continued. In a lower voice. Keeping his eye on Vemoth subdued now at the back of his church, *In the Twinking of an Eye.*

She slumped by the bird she'd drawn in the vestibule. It didn't seem scriptural. She mixed all kinds of things that didn't go together. *But didn't Jesus say the wheat and tares're together?* She answered Buddy Bob with scriptures that were smart.

But Buddy Bob Bill knew God wanted separation. That was what his whole Bible was about.

Sometimes she'd dig ditch lilies and plant them at the church until Brother Buddy Bob Bill mowed them down as he daydreamed of his next sermon while he mowed.

In the power of his might.

He did that a lot to Vemoth. But she was dazzled by his light.

Yes. They'd been where the pavement ends and they still kept going. Pushed on. Rolled up the windows in the heat to keep out the dust.

Vemoth wheezed.

In the name of Jesus, Buddy Bob said.

He hanged rusted nails on the TV aerial. Parts of old cars. Well, spark plugs, you know. The small parts. He got heaven on his television with snow and streaks and weather patterns over the earth and the units of demons hovering over Arkansas. That's how Pastor Brother Buddy Bob Billy Bub knew where they were. That's how he knew to keep going.

In the twinking of an eye we'll be lifted from this earth. If we don't jump when Satan says, *jump.*

If we don't do what everyone else did. If we didn't run with the demon crowd. If we thought on our own. There was a savior who bled to death and his blood was enough to cover all the EVIL in the earth. Let Vemoth hang that blasted Frida Kahlo all over the place.

Let her draw a bird that reached heaven.

Oh my Lord, he looked into his TV screen. Yes, he was seeing heaven! The walls of Jesus's room hung with Frida's painting. Vemoth's large bird flew everywhere. And there Frida was. Sitting with Diego, her love, who was an image of Christ! A perverted image of the real savior of Frida's heart, of course. Sanctified from all the hell-bent-on-earth things called to his kingdom of light. All those warty demons. It was too late for them, if they hadn't called Jesus, then nothing would work.

Holy Lord, there was Buddy Bob in his undershirt sitting on the couch of heaven. And Vemoth pouring out her love for Christ and Buddy Bob himself in her painting. And Buddy Bob was no better than Diego. None of them. No better than a *polly-lop.*

Yes, God opened the tuna can of Buddy Bob's evil little heart. Pried it loose with his can opener. God had a counter full of them. Just like the cafe. Open late. The fry cook with his frown. The waitress with her specials. She could bulge between the booths all she wanted. They were all in God's holy water. He was the celestial fry cook his spatulas flipping the stars. Yehovah. He was God Almighty. The Great Spam himself.

You reach for perfection you nail it to the cross it has to die you have to see Frida Kahlo walk across your path.

Then you take your way of thinking. Your will. Your ideas of the way things should hang. And let them go.

Satan had made him *jump!* when Buddy Bob Bill heard anything that didn't agree with him. God was trying to get him to be more accepting. Forgiving. Tolerant. Now there was a word to curl your toes.

But Buddy Bob had a right to his confusion. In the Old Testament God didn't want anything that wasn't of himself. The enemy tribes and their possessions had to be gotten rid of. Even the sheep and cattle had to be put to death.

But of the cities of these people which the Lord thy God doth give thee for an inheritance, thou shalt save alive nothing that breatheth, But thou shalt utterly destroy them; namely, the Hittites, and the Amorites, the Canaanites, and the Perizzites, the Hivites, and the Jebusites, as the Lord thy God hath commanded thee: That they teach you not to do after all their abominations, which they have done unto their gods; so should ye sin against the Lord your God. (Deuteronomy 20: 16–18.)

How many nights had Buddy Bob tuned Vemoth with a recitation of Numbers and Deuteronomy? The genealogies?

The roastings of the various burnt offerings? How often had Buddy Bob's congregation yawned and he had to crack the pulpit with his fist? Startling even the huge finch (?) in its mural?

And wide-eyed once again, they'd take in the gospel scriptures where the heavy spring of Satan's (SAYTUN'S!!) voice didn't work. Hallelujah. Their feet held steady. They were still. Yes. They were on the rock bottom of heaven. He sighed at the whiff of Vemoth's mind as she moved through the church subtle as the sound of her shoes. The painting of her bird reaching heaven. The heart of Buddy Bob Bill popping like a slice of cafe bread from the silver toaster.

And they utterly destroyed all that was in the city (Jericho), both man and woman, young and old, and ox, and sheep, and ass, with the edge of the sword. (Joshua 6:21.)

Yes, that was a picture of how the people would be destroyed from the earth in the time of the millenium to come.

Woah. What was Buddy Bob Bill saying? A picture? He actually wanted Vemoth to paint another mural? Possibly an *Armageddonian* series? War and more war. Hunger. Famine. Pestilence. Death. In the Bible it was around the corner. But *In the Twinking of an Eye* (with an eyeball painted on the church) his congregation was ready.

There would be people taken from the earth before the end. Believers whose feet were still. Didn't God promise in the Bible? Well. Get ready for departure. Get ready for the take.

They would leap up to heaven on large bird wings. They would fly on their faith. They would be forever with God in the hereafter while the dark waves washed over the earth.

She

She'd been on a wrong-way street and he'd been crossing at the corner. They fell in love while a horn in front of her honked. They were married in a month and moved into a brown house on the corner of Ashland. He wanted a moose head over the mantle. It was all there was in the room. And their love. She wanted him more all the time. She painted the kitchen white and glued a border of cherries on the wall. She felt his kisses on the back of her neck. They slept late on Saturday morning. By the time she bathed after they made love it was noon.

When the spring sun reached the south border of the cherries, she was pregnant. A daughter was born in November. The leaves were wet and stuck to the window of the hospital. She thought they were like the sweat of labor. She wanted to tell him, but he'd left the room.

The baby cried often at first. When her husband began his love, she'd feel the pull toward the baby. On Saturday morning she fed the baby and rocked her back to sleep before she returned to bed.

He bought her a porch swing for the brown house on the corner of Ashland. When her mother visited they watched the flat yard. Speaking sometimes.

Later she bought a sofa and chest of drawers. She found an old ottoman and upholstered it.

It was hard for him, she tried to think. He was a man who made love. He knew how to touch her. It must have driven him to others the way sometimes she had something she had to share with neighbors. She knew it first next door. Then there was a call. Later she imagined him stopping after work or spending his lunch hour. He was silent at night. Then somehow he disappeared. Taking the moose head from the living room. The portrait of Geronimo from the bedroom wall. Sudden as the horn in front of her when she saw him on the corner.

But this time he wasn't there. She was by herself.

The sun had come and gone several times across the cherries. They were faded but still red. Sometimes her neck would chill as if desiring his kisses. Sometimes she touched the back of her neck. Then she asked her daughter to. Several times after work. Her neck was stiff. Her daughter's small hands could feel like a kiss. *Just touch me there*, she said, and her daughter would climb behind her on the chair and rub the back of her neck.

Just kiss me there, she said. And the daughter would rub and kiss her neck.

She'd close her eyes and remember him. Sometimes now she slept with her daughter. The desire for love was lovely and white and blossomed. But later it became red and round with a hard little seed and a stem. Sometimes she was her own lover. Sometimes there were other men. But it was never the same.

He had made her feel like no one else could. She desired him in the night. She thought of him in the day. If he'd just come and love her again. One night she dreamed of a huge cherry nearly rolling down a hill. The next night she called him, but another woman came to the phone.

Touch me, she said to her daughter. *Let me show you. There. Yes. Inside. Where it's wet. More of your fingers.* She asked more. She only wanted him to touch her. Her husband had known how to make her desire.

If the child refused, she took her hand and moved it the way she wanted. If the child cried, she had to sleep on the hardwood floor. If she was difficult, the mother withheld her breakfast. She told the child stories of why she did it. She sent cherries in her lunch box. On Saturday she saw gorillas if she'd touch her mother that morning. Even the monkeys in the zoo with their red bottoms had love. It was something like when two tongues came together. Or when two fists.

Sometimes he came to take the child for a Sunday. The woman tried to get him to stay. But he had his hand on the door. When he left she felt the pull of him away from her. She felt the first downpour of winter when the white snow blossomed in the streets.

She shoveled the walk after the storms. Then she lay on the bed thinking of his love. Hadn't he said how lovely women were as he loved her? Hadn't she met his mother once? She'd come the summer the daughter was three. She remembered how graceful she'd been in a white tulle dress.

Yes, it was her own mother she remembered as sensual. A woman's body was like a face. The two round breasts of the eyes. The mouth. And the little navel of the nose. Her mother'd had an angry life with her father. Had probably never known. She wanted to know love. And she wanted her daughter to know love. To feel.

Here touch me, she said. *Let's put our tongues together. Let's make a pact.*

It was more often now she asked the daughter for her favors. They needed no one else. Hadn't the man always left?

She grew more insular. Isolated. She no longer wanted her mother to visit. She asked her not to come. She seemed to remember as a child the fear of being devoured.

Often now she worked in her house. Upholstering. If it were uncomplicated. Her husband gave her money for the child.

When it was warm, she sat on the porch swing waiting for her daughter after school.

She put Jesus on the wall where Geronimo had been. A landscape in the place of the moose head in the living room. She put an *Upholstery* sign in her yard because she loved the fabric with its nubs and knots, its differences passing like a parade.

At supper they talked in the white room with its border of cherries.

Sometimes he came to get the girl on Sundays and asked if anything was wrong. She seemed distant. Unreachable. There were some Sundays he didn't come at all. Then she walked with her daughter to the neighborhood park. If other girls came around them, they pretended they couldn't talk.

The girl was in the fourth grade and the mother wanted to be with her all the time. She thought of a job at school. She could be the one who spooned out cherries at lunch. Or the one who took roll. She could do her upholstering in the evening. She even thought sometimes she could go to upholstery school. Hadn't she always wanted to do something like that?

How often now he made her think of the gorillas. How she loved the zoo. More than the monkeys. She thought of the gorillas. Did they know the secret of night when they lay down together? Here put your tongue to me. Let me show you. There.

The girl didn't fuss anymore. She was quiet as the zoo on a chilled autumn day.

If the girl wanted her lunch money in a purse her mother made of upholstery fabric, she had to obey. That was the law of the house. To follow her mother's desires and not fight against them.

Now they had a birthday party in November before a snow. The girl had a new dress with presents on the table and candles in her red cake. A card from both grandmothers. Her father would come later but this was a day for the girl and her mother. The landscape on the mantle. The sofa reupholstered and the new chair in the living room. In one of the presents was a flounce for the bed.

The mother wanted her now all the time. Later that evening when he came with a box she felt desire for him but didn't ask him to stay.

She was already thinking of her daughter in junior high, riding the bus far way from her during the day.

One day as she worked with her tucking tool, her upholstery tacks and rubber hammer, the school called and asked if she could come and see them. If she could come and talk. *Tomorrow at two?*

They sat in the room where she came. She didn't think they should ask such things. It was between her and her daughter. It was what her daughter chose to do. If she didn't want to sleep on the floor hard as the pit of a cherry.

She had shoveled the walk even when it hardly snowed. She had thought about the monkeys. How long had it been since she'd seen them? *Remember the zoo on Saturdays?* She said when they brought her daughter into the room. *Didn't we have a nice time?*

A Woman Who Sewed for Me
a Dress That Sleeves Didn't Fit

I don't like to remember sewing class. It was always something I couldn't do. Like the rest of school, for that matter. I don't want to look at it on my own. So I bring in someone else to hide the crooked seams.

Fayfern, for instance.

Though she's really me.

The part of me that couldn't sew.

She was a *zippo* with the machine.

Doing what I couldn't.

There was this fashion show in junior high. We had to make our clothes. I made some horrid outfit I had to wear. When I walked down the runway I wished I were dead.

Years later, I can look back and walk down that runway with my words. As though I were *hotstuff*. Because a fictive is there.

Or the pain of my rebirth.

Fayfern with my own voice *bleeting* through. You can tell where.

Up near the sheep station when I was in Australia. (I appear in a sheep-suit.)

Baa.

It seems I can only tell a little at a time.

My father was transferred to several packing houses in the Midwest.

When I was in sixth grade I moved from a small school named Flackville to a large consolidated one. At the new school, the other girls were already at their machines.

I came late to sewing.

Fayfern made her first jean skirt from her brother's old jeans. You know how you open up the inside double seam.

Like untangling barbed wire.

When I tried it I bent the needle, but the shoe repairman had an industrial machine. He sewed the front seams together, then the back.

Maybe I should patent it, my sewing teacher said.

I wore my jean skirt like a welder's apron. It felt like a metal plate around my legs.

I was somewhere in junior high when I saw sewing as a religious conversion.

> *Now there was at Joppa a certain disciple, named Dorcas*
> *... and all the widows stood weeping, and showing the coats*
> *and garments which Dorcas made.*
>
> ACTS 9:36–39

Fayfern knew it every time she had her foot on the footfeed. She had a spirit in her hands.

She made morrals (feed bags around the neck)

Navajo gear bags

chaps for skirts

chinks (short chaps)

denim knee patches (for skirts).

Dorcas was her vison quest.

Thread was her medicine bundle.

I called my place in the sewing room, *The Body Shop.*

I had a magazine picture of a red vintage Ford truck with a Navajo blanket over the seat and a leather steering wheel.

Forgetting I didn't have anywhere to go.

Forgetting I didn't have anything to go in.

At times my needle broke the sound barrier.

At times my needle plodded like the old tractor in my grandfather's field.

I felt the fabric join like man and wife.

Anything to cover my body-suit.

Baa.

I told stories to the pieces I made.

How they were a testament.

It didn't matter if anyone laughed.

Trail blazers, I called them.

She has bobbin eyes, I said of the teacher.

Yes, I had a tongue like a footfeed telling stories to hold my life together. At the table in the sewing room with the other girls. The place buzzy as bees in the summer pasture's clover.

Now I wanted to sew a dress to cover my sheep-suit.

All it would take was a simple resurrection from the dead.

> *Then the soldiers, when they had crucified Jesus, took his garments, and made four parts, to every soldier a part; and also his coat. Now the coat was without seam, woven from the top throughout.*
>
> JOHN 19:23

I wanted my sheep dress without seams like Jesus's coat. A white canvas dress wrapped like a teepee around me.

I don't think even Dorcas could have done it.

I made a pattern from newspaper.

Maybe like God forming Eve from a rib. His newspapers laid out in the yard in Eden. Hoping for a windless day. Straight pins in his mouth. Making darts. Some hairs from animals he'd already made.

One girl had a stud-er.

I could have glittered my sheep dress with silver studs. But I decided I'd make the dress with sequins.

Me and my (powwow) Singer.

I think I was obsessed.

In the night I dreamed I was the girl who became a sewing machine. My teeth biting the sacraments of cloth together.

In the rapture I wore my rizzly sheep dress with a bell around my neck.

Sheep cape, they called it.

Sheep coat.

Sometimes it seems I can only talk of myself in terms of another.

Sometimes I walk at the edge of the summer's-clover field when something appears gathering nothing into an image.

A sheen.

A sheep dress of the purest light.

Lamb of God.

(I try to uncover myself. As a sheep, I could only stand a two-log fire.)

Jesus, you're the sheep catcher, I said.

There's a place where the perfect sewing machine sews without seams. A machine that does sequins, zippers, windows.

A machine that heals as it sews.

There He Is Again

You learn to read you won't
remember nothing

REGINALD GIBBONS
Sweetbitter

There were the monks' cells at San Marco in Florence I would
remember I said. *The rooms cold and drafty in the north of Italy. The*
walls austere but for the frescos by Fra Angelico. About the Man who
tours Italy. On a donkey. With His Mother. On the Cross. He shows
up every town. Lifting His arms. Standing on His toes for as long as
He can. The red holes in His hands. The blood-drops on His side.

Everywhere. Him Born. Crucified.

After the San Marco museum, we walk along the Arno and
sit in a cafe near the Ponte Vecchio. The bridge with shops on it
like a row of beehives from the distance.

In the end you were probably glad to get out of the earth I say.
There was so much looking forward to it. You see the adoring saints.
The angel with its backpack. You see everyone with that thing, that
nimbus behind their head, that aura in their face they had to push out
of the way if they turned around to look backward it was in their face.

You see the martyrs burned at the stake in the high air. A slow
burn to death. Oh God Your Truth Is Word.

As I talk, my husband, Philip, who is distant as the beehives, watches the tourists that crowd past our table. He sees a
couple—Dakota, he thinks. *Casino money*, he says. I keep
thinking of San Marco. The fresco in each cell. The one of the

monk with blood on his bald head as if scalped. Later an angel with hatchet in another cell. The bare stone floors. Stone walls. Christ the Durable Death. The One who Lasted.

Philip's eye is always everywhere else. He has always moved independent of me.

Yes. It's Christ's whose Travel we're under. His Story Everywhere. *It's what I believe we're born to decide* I say. *You feel it more sometimes when a truck loaded with fertilizer and fuel oil drives in front of a building. Some sort of detonator is sparked and the front of the building falls.*

It's because I have to find something other than Philip to believe. I have to find more than the disruptions of the past.

Sometimes I feel the weight of too much happening. I feel everything I've come from. Every place I'm going.

You read too many newspapers, Philip says. *I told you you'd go crazy hurrying from Duomo to Duomo. You can only walk through so many cathedrals and steep vineyards and rolling Italy hills.*

Christ in Rome. Venice. Florence.

Christ on his motorcycle.

Christ dragging the heavy Cross behind Him.

Christ hydroplaning.

Wearing Italian leather.

Christ in the Holy Rubble.

As I talk, Philip thinks for a moment he sees someone he knows. He raises his arm but realizes he's mistaken.

What would they be doing here anyway? I ask.

He frowns and remembers we were talking. *What are we born to decide?* He asks.

Whether to believe Christ or not. How long have the missionaries been at it?

Philip looks toward the Ponte Vecchio. *Believe Him about what?*

About His death for our sins, I say with the sun in my eyes. *I'm realizing I want more of Him in my life. We've been blessed, Philip. I want to do something.*

What do you want?

These Christian paintings have made me want more religion in my life. I want to go to church—to take part. To have it Mean-something.

Philip takes another drink of his espresso. The wind blows his napkin and he grabs it.

We've been married a long time, I continue. *We go to church. We're from a Christian country. You can't leave me alone in my recognition of this. You treat me like I have snakes in my hair. I have to be one for whom He died.*

It's why there's more women in church.

The sky turns fireworks above the river. With the traffic noise and horns between them.

In Rome there was the Sistine.

In Venice there was Christ parasailing the waves over the shifting and sinking of St. Mark's parquet floors. In Venice there was the *Madonna e Santi* by Giovanni Da Bologna, circa 1390. He was the Baby sucking His thumb. In *Politicco* by Michele Giambono, it looked as if He were the Baby reading. Then where was it? The Baby holding His Mother's thumb with cow and sheep's breath visible on Him.

The whole landscape of the Bible we carry in our imagination is painted here in Italy. *They don't have to hold onto what they can't see,* I say. *I think we lose something from our head when we can see it.*

Philip doesn't seem to be listening.

But the visible forms have reminded me of what I need to hold onto—because of the hurt—the abuse in my childhood.

You weren't abused as a child.

I was. I suppressed the memories.

It's that group you got into—that corkscrewed bunch of women—imagining their hurts. It's not possible. You had a normal childhood. Your father's tenderness with his garden. Philip said. *Come on, Frances.*

You also abused me.

I've never touched you.

Your neglect and derision are abuse.

Then don't leave yourself open. You invite it. It's in the subconscious of every woman. We've tweaked her out behind the bushes of her childhood.

There are stories that go around. I say. *Part of the myth of location that transcends geographies. You've heard the story of the woman with cockroaches in her hair. It's just another surburban mythology.*

It's the woman abused, Philip adds. *Because of the old guilt myth of Eve. Abuse is the just rewards of her.*

That's Medusa. Who had snakes on her head. The eeeevil woman who had to be killed because she was evil.

I wouldn't go that far, Philip answers. *But it's what's in a woman's head,* he says.

Well, sew my mouth shut so I can't speak. Sew my eyebrows together so I'll frown.

Philip looks at me and I know I'll alienate him more if I keep on. I say, *the yellow walls in Florence are calmer. Why are we arguing? Look at the narrow cobblestone streets. The lace curtains in the cafe windows near the Ponte Vecchio. The tile roofs of the steep houses along the winding Arno. I could be pulling weeds in our yard, but we're sitting along the river in Florence.*

Philip isn't looking at the river. He asks the waïter for the bill.

I'm just saying I want to know more of Christ. It's what I've discovered on our trip.

We walk along the Uffizi before heading north to Milan the next day to take a plane back to America.

We pass the statue of Dante with the cap with earflaps on his head.

The shops of bright Murano Italian glass.

Indigo as in Diego comes to mind, I guess, as in Rivera, his hand-washed workers working in the mural.

Orange as the sound of argument.

Yellow, a yell oh at who oh you oh.

As we walk, the sky separates into darkness. I think I hear an echo of the explosion I read in the papers.

We walk to *La Pentola dell'oro Firenze.* A restaurant where we have dinner.

Philip orders *La Cucina Medicea* for us. From the *composizioni vegetariane e piatti unici integrati,* he decides on *L' orto di dehetra.* From the *dolci e frutta,* he chooses *Le classico Torte di Mele delle vecchie zia zitella co'i' doltoze.* I have always trusted his taste.

Philip eats in silence with his food. I'm afraid if he showed himself he'd disappear.

Not everyone was evangelized by the missionaries that passed through the tribe. He finally says.

There are times I feel invisible with Philip. I want to do something to get his attention. He is growing away from me and I don't know what to do about it. I am realizing maybe nothing can be done. My faith that we will be renewed may have to be replaced by the faith I will survive on my own without him. I hate feeling *unvaluable.* I have felt it with him a long time. I want to be dear to him.

My head swarms with bees. My eyes feel round as cherries. My tongue snakes like an orange river in the cellar of the restaurant where we eat downstairs.

You know when the atmosphere has changed and will never be the way it was again.

But all things are possible. All things are in gear. Because of the Man whose Name was Transformation. The Man whose Name was Travel.

He's in heaven up there now. I know it. The Solace of the nimbused angels. Maybe faith is what I'll hold in my head. Stronger because I can't see the way ahead.

America's First Parade

1

She was in her red truck with the *Indian Territory* bumper sticker. She stopped in front of Redland's Cafe on Muskogee Street in Tahlequah, Oklahoma, where she was part owner. She saw her truck reflected in the plate-glass window smooth as a butter knife.

"Mom." He turned down the radio. "You're grinding gears."

"Is that what that noise is?"

Some boys revved their car next to her at the second stoplight.

"Everybody's mother drives a station wagon. A sedan."

"I got a deal." She started with a jerk.

"Grow up, Mom."

She pulled away from the stoplight in the dust of the boys next to her. She slowed at the next corner, but not enough. She made the turn a little fast. He opened the door.

"I'm getting out, Mom, if you don't slow down."

She slowed and the truck jumped. "What's the matter?"

"You got to shift."

"Again?"

"You got to shift all the time, Mom. Why didn't you take me with you to look at cars? Here—look. Hold the brake down. Put your foot on the clutch." He shifted to show her. "First. Second. Third. Reverse. Neutral." A car behind them honked. "Why didn't you get an automatic?"

"I want to feel the power in my hands." She started up this time without a hitch. She touched her finger to her tongue and then the gearshift. "*SSSSSSSSSSS.*"

They were quiet for several blocks through Tahlequah, then the woman said, "I see them sometimes—"

"Who?"

"The spirits."

The son didn't say anything.

"Sometimes they pull up next to me and I can see them from the corner of my eye, but when I turn to look, they drive off."

Her son looked out the window.

"Sometimes I hear their voices."

"The spirits?"

"No, the ones who walked the trail. I think I hear them walking. Or I think sometimes I hear an old ball game in the field. Ever hear them? When you're camping?"

"No."

"Hunting?"

"No."

"When you got a girl in the woods?"

"Mom."

"You aren't listening hard enough." She ground the gears again, then pulled away from a stop with another jerk.

"Yellow Bud's garage is about to close." He waved as they passed. "I'll let him know he's in business."

"He's the one who sold me the truck."

"Yellow Bud? Shit, Mom. Will you slow down?"

"I was driving before you were born."

"You ain't made a lot of progress."

"I hear the voices sometimes in the engine." She turned down a road on the edge of town. "I hear them sometimes where the sky comes down to the land, with a few trees and a little brush to hold up the clouds."

He looked at the trees that passed above them.

"America's first parade was the forced march of our Cherokee people from the southeast. Some of the parade reached Oklahoma. Some of it left the earth and went into the sky."

She stopped talking for a moment and looked at the leaves reflected in the window glass. A hawk flew through the trees. "Sometimes I can't keep their voices straight. They slip around in my head."

"Isn't that where they really are?"

She crossed a narrow bridge over a creek. One of her son's friends passed from the other direction. She heard his loud radio. The son reached over to the steering wheel, honked, waved at him. The car stopped. Her son got out of the truck and went to his friend's car. They drove off.

With a jump of the truck, the woman started back toward Tahlequah. At another one-lane bridge, she slowed and didn't shift in time. The truck jumped again and died. She couldn't get it started. She sat on the road alone, listening to the birds and insects. She felt the hot wind on her face and neck. She wiped her sweat.

Soon the spirits came. Their faces were painted red. They wore masks on the back of their heads. But this time the woman didn't see them.

"What do we know about engines?" One of the spirits asked. "All we can do is drive."

Another answered, "We can't do anything anyway."

"Why not?"

"She hasn't asked."

"Maybe she doesn't believe."

"She can't see us yet."

"She's seen us before. Why not now?"

"She isn't paying attention."

"How are we supposed to fix a truck?"

"It's a matter of relationship. Cycles. Harmony. Just like it's always been."

The woman opened the hood of the truck. Hummed a spirit-song.

"She's warming up."

"Just like butter on hot bread."

"I don't want engine grease on my hands."

"Find a rag."

"Tell the engine stories," the spirit said to the woman as though she could hear his voice. "Maybe America's first parade was a trail of spirits from the sky to the earth. Maybe we came to look things over. To see if we could sweep up. Get the people going again."

The woman fiddled with the engine. She told it a story that glistened like the silvery line of a slug across her step at night. To get the engine off track. To bypass its troubles. And because of the story and the woman's tinkering, there was an alignment between the spirit realm and the engine. The truck snorted on the road. She got in. It was something Yellow Bud would have to fix, but for now the truck started.

"WUUUUUUH!" She let out a war cry and drove down the road. Yes, she thought, *women were the warriors of the world.*

2

"There's a plate on the table." She said as she stirred the beans.

"I just ate," he answered.

"The truck died after you left, but I got it started. You could help more. Mow the lawn. Work on the truck. Go to the grocery once in a while."

"I don't want to," her son said.

"I don't either."

"There aren't any jobs."

"You could work at Redland's."

"I don't want to."

"I know, but you could pick up around here."

"It's not my place."

"Get your own then."

"Soon as I get some bread."

"The last time you got into it with bills and rent and utilities you couldn't get out."

"Yeah, I ain't been able to do anything right yet. Why start now?" He went to his room.

She sat at the table eating the beans by herself.

Her son woke with a dream. He said, "Mom, they're surrounding us they will take us they will march us on a trail."

She went into his room. "It's already happened," she said. "It's your great-great-great-grandparents. Over one hundred years ago. The story works at night. It's carried in the storage room in our heads. You hear them," she said.

3

She sat in Yellow Bud's while he worked on the engine of her truck. His garage was a small stucco building at the end of Muskogee Street, painted half turquoise / half yellow with spirit signs around the doors.

She offered her truck some tobacco. She offered a prayer. She had the power of the spirits. She had the visions of the ancestors. She had a truck. She'd received part ownership of Redland's Cafe when she divorced, though she felt it all should be hers because her father had started the cafe. But her father had been a vacant booth behind her. Now she was slowly buying her former husband's half from him.

After she left Yellow Bud's, she saw her son on the street. She honked at him, and her truck bucked. It would never drive smoothly.

Her son said, "I asked Yellow Bud why I hadn't seen that truck before. He told me he got it someplace else. I think you got took, Mom."

"It isn't the first time."

Sometimes she saw the spirits, she told her son as they drove through Tahlequah. Driving around with masks on the back of their heads. They looked like they were looking at you, but they were facing the other way.

Her son looked at her as if she threw him something he could catch in one hand. Maybe even backhanded. She wanted him to hear a noise in the engine so he could tell Yellow Bud. He got out of the truck at the next light.

4

Now she had flames painted on the fenders of her truck. Yellow Bud's hand was shaky, but the flames were there, jittery as if the wind flicked them.

5

The lights that let her go sometimes stopped her with their yellow-jacket yellow. But she was in her truck with flames on the front fenders. Once her life had been the size of the hole in the top of the glass milk bottles they used to have in the cafe. The memories of her father still smoldered.

Her father had worn a mask all those years. She'd never known his feelings until he wasn't there anymore.

Why hadn't she thought of her son when she looked at trucks? Somehow they always just missed. If he'd just eaten, she had fixed his supper by the time he got back. If he was hungry, there would be nothing in the house to eat. She could flare with her intentions. But the fire was never there.

If she turned the mask around and looked back. All of life was only a parade of masks. Acting as if they had concern for one another. As if they belonged together, but they were only cardboard and paint. That's what they were.

How could she love her son when she hadn't been loved by her father? Or by her mother, either. She was always grieving over her father's love of other women.

Where did love come from? What was it? It was bright as the candles from all the birthdays her father had missed, whatever it was.

But her father'd only acted as if he loved her. He'd been a parade of absences through her birthdays. Now the flames were all the birthday candles on the front fenders of her truck.

Even the country was caught up in its mask of history. The trail of the ancestors no one wanted to talk about. What had happened was only partly known.

She paraded through her life. She'd acted as if she loved her husband. She acted as if she loved the customers at Redland's. The women who ordered cottage cheese, and took up tables and booths in the noon rush hour. The *old wheezer* she could hardly understand. He would gag trying to say something, and whoever he was talking to couldn't under-stand, and would ask him to repeat. Then he'd choke out his sentence again, while the customers stopped eating and looked at him.

What were the spirits saying? She had to look back to name what happened before she could go on? She had to look back at nothing. She had to look back so nothing could take her from behind.

Why couldn't she understand?

She saw them sometimes, actually saw the spirits, but she had to figure out what they meant. Why did she have to determine what they meant? They couldn't quite get through? Or didn't want to. Or wanted to make her work? She thought they were like her father.

The cottonwoods fluttered like milk beyond the window of her truck. The leaves told her a story, but no one listened to the leaves. Each day the earth told a story but no one heard. The noise of traffic was louder.

Maybe there had to be space before the time to say it comes. A woman driving up a long hill.

That's the way it was. Always uphill.

She sat at the stoplight now with the spirits jumping in their truck next to her. Had they been to Yellow Bud's too?

They took off in a buzz. Their truck was ahead of her. The spirits were in it. She could see the faces of their masks.

If they kept that up, they'd need a fuzz buster.

6

In Redland's Cafe, the cook fried her a Redland's burger while she worked on payroll and receipts, checked supplies in the storage room.

There was an opened letter from the city of Tahlequah, and her son left a note saying he was moving in with a girl.

Well, she had to have space.

Space.

But it was all right here in Tahlequah.

The cook had a kerchief around his neck. She could give him a ride in her truck, but he had his eye on someone.

Hadn't one of the spirits worn a handkerchief? She looked around the cafe. Maybe they were at the table by the window. All sorts of their folded language like napkins dropped on the floor.

She remembered how she'd sat in the cafe as a girl watching her father with his snakeskin boots and silver belt buckle. His shirt with cuff ornaments and silver tabs on the collar. He'd been the Chief at Redland's, but he'd lost interest. Didn't watch the books. The waitresses took more than their share. Then her mother had kept books, sometimes waited tables. But she'd started drinking and he'd gone on to other women.

She had tried to hold her head up at school. All the girls knew.

She and her husband had started over. Bought the cafe again. Her husband had saved it from loss. It was theirs. Their son had crawled on the floor and sat on customers' laps.

Then her husband's interest had moved on.

The place seemed suddenly smaller. She was a butter knife that couldn't cut anything. A yellow-jacket sting. A mask on the back of her head with holes for eyes. Just eat her Redland's whizzburger w/jalepeno and a piece of homemade pie.

Read the *Cherokee Observer*.

Look at the note from her son again.

But not the opened letter. It would be from the building inspector saying a leak needed repair, or from the health inspector saying something had been left uncovered or there was a parade of ants across the floor.

She remembered she'd ridden a horse in a parade on Muskogee Street though town. She remembered the hat with a pull-string under her chin. She'd wanted her mother to cut the string off, but she said the hat would blow away in the wind, and she'd lose it during the parade.

She remembered the first time she'd watched her reflection in the plate-glass window at Redland's. It was her mask. She had to make sure she was there.

The buildings crowded the narrow main street of town. The street names were written in Cherokee underneath the English. The bank and hardware were also in Cherokee.

Why did everyone seem to come and go in her life, leaving their crumbs on her plate, their spots of grease on the napkins? But she carried on. Yes, she thought, *women were sometimes the warriors of the world.*

7

"Aren't you going to look at the letter?" The cook asked her. "It's been here a week."

She unfolded the letter from the city of Tahlequah.

"Blast it!" She clapped the letter shut as if it were a fly. "He can't do that!" The inspector was on her tail all the time. Her father had slept with his mother thirty years ago, and he couldn't forget. Or his mother wouldn't let him. The frypan! He was caught on revenge. Every piece of lint, every zone he marked. Inspecting it with his telescope. His magnifying glass.

She was not going to get angry again. The health inspector had found another code violation. She stomped from Redland's. Jerked her truck from its place on Muskogee Street. It died at the first light.

Cars honked.

As she tried to start the truck again, she thought she could tell herself a story to bypass her troubles. They could all sit in the middle of the street and tell old stories. Why were they still honking? Couldn't they see she was having trouble?

On the road, she'd heard old ball games in a field. She'd heard the ancestors. Spirits. The birds. The wind. The sky. Why not in town?

One car went around her, the driver shaking his fist, saying something. The others were more patient because they knew her.

Soon she got the truck started again. With a jerk of the gearshift, she was driving through the brush fire of her anger. She could smell burning grass.

But it was her truck, smoke coming from the engine.

Yes, the truck had come from somewhere else. Across a trail halfway across the country, with moons floating above it like cab lights. Two suns for headlights. Campfires for taillights.

Yellow Bud had painted it red. Who knew what it was underneath?

Smoke billowed now over the hood of her truck.

It was a spirit truck. It had driven all that way. Nine hundred miles on a long trail over 150 years ago. That's why the truck didn't work. It had come that far.

What had the ancestors thought when a truck picked them up? Did they know they'd stepped into the next world?

Suddenly her son was there. "Stop," he said. "Mom, move over. You got to get the truck off the street." He shifted the truck, and with another jump, pulled it over to the curb and shut off the engine.

One car passed, yelling something she didn't understand.

"I'm going to tell Yellow Bud to take this truck back and get you one that's been around here, one I know who's had it."

"I want this truck."

"Mom, it don't run. It's a killer truck. It would be quicker to drop a match in the gas tank."

"It's been in a parade of history."

"We'll all drive in a line through Tahlequah so your next truck will have parade time too."

"It won't be the same."

"Nothing ever is. Get used to it. Yellow Bud will paint you more flames, or I'll wring his greasy nose ring."

She sat in the smoking truck with her son. People were still standing around, though the smoke only trailed from the engine now.

Her son got out. "Guess we can open the hood."

The people moved back. The spirits stood by him holding handkerchiefs over their noses, shaking their heads at the people always out of whack.

The other spirits had their fingers under their noses.

What was love? She'd always wondered. It was the son who looked at the engine of her truck shaking his head.

It was the struggle to live.

It was when she could break through to the spirit world. She wasn't really doing it by herself. The ancestors had gone before her. She had more help than she knew.

No, she thought, *women were never the warriors of the world.*

The spirits came closer to the truck, to see what could cause a campfire in an engine.

It was a small imperfect world, they told her, *where things were tenuous at best. You hung on and acted like you knew what was happening. You did what could be done. You came as close to understanding what went on as you could.*

The woman sat in her red truck painted with flames at the end of Muskogee Street in Tahlequah, Oklahoma. Yes, the spirits checked their state map. It was Oklahoma.

One of them still stood by her son with a foot on the fender. Some of them sat next to her.

But no, you couldn't tell her anything.

8

She was at a window table in Redland's Cafe reading a postcard from her former husband with her yellow-jacket eyes. It was postmarked, Georgia.

Duck or venison, or sausage of somesort. Amish blue cheese. Pickled grapes. Purple potatoes. Beets. Plums. Applewood smoke. Yam mash w/ pearl onions. Butternut squash.

Where'd he get such ideas? If there was an out-of-the-way cafe somewhere, he'd find it. But this wasn't an ordinary postcard from a cafe. For a moment, another world opened to her. She thought of black vinegar and sea scallops. Jalepeno and chipotle pepper. Picked ginger relish and oven-dried pineapple. Wasabi mustard sauce. She held his postcard, feeling her folded wings.

When she looked up from the postcard, she saw her son's friends across the street. Bib. Fill. Jowan. Harford. Sometimes when she watched them, she could see the ancestors crossing the hot traffic of an Oklahoma summer. But back then, the ancestors had walked through the cold. She knew they'd made it to the new territory; she knew it because of the boys. They were the image of their great-great-grandfathers walking, an assemblage of voices in different groups passing.

She lifted her hand as they waved from the street.

9

Her son took her to Gillette's car lot. Now she had another truck. This time, an automatic. The parade went on—the vehicle just changed. She hummed it a spirit song. She offered it tobacco.

She got a new *Indian Territory* bumper sticker.

And what was Indian Territory? She thought. A greasy place on the menu where you could slide over where you didn't want to stop.

10

Her son's girlfriend was a Gillette. Her father had the car lot where her son had got her truck. She had to say she liked the truck; she would take it to Yellow Bud for a tattoo, and she'd like it better. She'd also find it a bumper sticker.

Her red truck with flames sat behind her house with an old convertible her father once drove.

They had the same name, Janet. Janet Gillette. It sounded like the make of a car.

The girl called her Mom also.

She looked at her, but the girl didn't flinch.

The girl's parents never missed church, she'd heard, but their daughter was living with her son.

How did they manage that?

Now the new red truck had the name, *Redlands*, on it. Mr. Gillette and her son said if she'd put the name of the cafe on it, she could claim it on her taxes.

That afternoon, she had a naming ceremony for her truck. Then she took it to Yellow Bud for a small tattoo, a spirit sign, just under the doorknob. She got to him just before he closed his garage.

11

She had another postcard from her former husband. *Fried pork, baked chicken, frybread, corn bread, brown beans, slaw, wildberry cobbler.*

"U-ne-la-nv-hi, Father God," she said.

The cook looked at her through the window of the kitchen. She let him stare. Cooks who stayed longer than two weeks were hard to find.

And wear a ribbon dress made of calico print. Her husband finished. His next idea was a Cherokee menu in the cafe.

She nearly had him paid off for his half; another five years at most. He was not coming back.

12

"O-si-yo!" Her son greeted her in Cherokee.

"Where's your girl?" She asked, thinking then of *O-si-yo*, for a menu cover.

He picked up the postcard.

"Let me guess," she said. "You won't do nothing to help."

Now he picked up a piece of bread.

"I have my house to myself now. I'm getting used to loneliness. I'm getting used to not having your mess."

"Mom," he paused, "how's the new truck?"

"Sitting in the drive. Waiting to go. I can't get used to its impatience. I heard it calling me just last night. You sure you don't want it?"

"I drive my own truck. A demo. A spitfire turquoise. I'm driving it long as I stay enrolled at Northeastern."

"I thought you flunked out of there."

"Mr. Gillette got me back in. I'm taking accounting, applying it to his books at the car lot."

13

It was her theory of frying. Just get it done.

She had taken out a book of old recipes from the library at Northeastern State.

Squirrel stew w/ lima beans.

Woodcock.

Pigeon.

Stewed coot.

Venison.

Rabbit and hare
hang with head down when skinned and dressed
blood collected under the ribs
use for gravies, sauces, and stews.

Casserole of pintails.

Woodchuck.

Groundhog
remove fat glands under front legs and along spine
because of the sour taste
remove also sinews, second skin, and nerves.

Milkweed casserole
    flour, milk, butter, bread crumbs, salt and pepper.
    She had that.
    Knotweed.
    Cattail.
    Blueberry.
    Sumac.

She thought of the story of the woman who married an owl, though he looked like a man when she married him. At night when he hunted, all he brought back was crawfish, lizards, and moths. One night she followed him, and saw him turn into an owl. When he came back, she hit him away from the house with a stick.

Her son had his father and grandfather's handsomeness, but not their smoothness. He was eratic, but he was always around. She usually knew where he was, even when he was someplace else.

Now Janet Gillette had him back at the state university in Tahlequah, taking accounting. He had a purpose. Why hadn't he wanted to use his accounting at Redland's Cafe?

She closed the library book of recipes. She was going through old papers and scattered postcards when she came across the deed to the cafe signed, Bill and Janet Wills. She marked his name off, leaving hers alone. She would get it done. Just like her theory of frying.

14

Her son was going to marry Janet Gillette, probably the first of several wives he would have. She guessed so anyway. They would have an outdoor ceremony at the Gillette's, and a party afterwards at Fill's, one of her son's friend's.

She still had to pay for her truck.

As the weeks went by, she was invited to parties and dinners and giveaway ceremonies for her son and Miss J. Gillette.

She came and went at the cafe. She had a letter from her former husband saying he'd been invited to the wedding. She bought a dress. The Gillettes and their friends had vans and large houses. All the economic stability.

The day of the wedding, she heard a hymn in Cherokee. The wide backyard of the Gillette's house was decorated with old ceremonial brush arbors. Ribbons danced from the trees. She caught her breath as she walked into the yard. Something from her past, from the past of the tribe, stopped her. A connection had been made, and she was not aware of it until now. Traditions had been remembered. The past honored.

Jowan walked her into the yard among the wedding guests with her former husband following. Her former husband with his two-tone heart. She stood by him through the ceremony.

Janet wore a white linen dress hanging with white ribbons. The attendants wore traditional ribbon dresses, but instead of the calico the Cherokee women had seen the settlers' wives wear, the girls had dresses of the palest turquoise linen. There was something about them that made a lump in her throat.

She felt like she wore a mask backwards.

Her son had told her that he and Janet Gillette would camp out in the Arbuckle Anticline in southern Oklahoma. *U-ne-la-nv-hi*, she thought. It was where she and his father had camped.

Maybe they didn't always miss.

She told the spirits to go with them.

106

In the Arbuckle Mountains, the ancient bedrock had buckled. Over the centuries, the bowed rock was exposed by wind and water erosion. Then the highway cut through the hills, exposing them further.

She felt her own bedrock exposed. She wanted to cry. But in her bedrock, there was more anger than sorrow.

Why didn't she have that quietness her grandmother had? Why hadn't she seen the renewal in the Cherokee? She had that restlessness she'd seen in her father, but she couldn't blame it on him. The only thing she didn't want was to stand still. The anger was at herself. The guilt. She belonged to the generations between her grandma and her children, who were finding their way back to what she and her parents had thrown away. Now it was facing her in its loveliness.

Not everyone had thrown it away. The Gillettes had been married nearly thirty years. They had held their lives together.

She thought of her grandma. Maybe she'd go back and try to find her place sometime. A few miles southwest of Stilwell.

She returned to her house after the wedding. She had friends. She could be with any of them. Her former husband would have stayed the night. Why was she alone? She'd lived in Tahlequah all her life. She could start a recipe club, she thought. She'd invent the *I-took-the-wrong-rocky-road-cake*. She'd eat it and have it both, she thought, and finally, she cried.

15

She was busy in the cafe for several weeks after the wedding. She was trying to decide what changes to make, though she knew she wouldn't make any. Not then, anyway. But she liked to think about changing the cafe. And she liked to think about finding her grandma's old place again.

Any of the single men she knew would be glad to go with her, but she wanted to drive by herself in her truck, and poke in the weeds and find the rocks that marked the corner of her grandma's place.

Sometimes she had stayed with her grandma when her mother was gone with some man. She remembered her grandma had lye soap, and her skin would be red and chapped. She remembered her grandma had made her a bed-sack of moss, which they boiled, then dried in the sun. At first it was hard and had scratched, but soon it softened, and her bed was like sleeping on deerskin.

In the early days, the government had given the Cherokee rations of flour, sugar, salt, beans, and coffee, as long as it lasted, then her grandma made the coffee from parched grain and bark, sometimes burnt sweet potatoes. She'd made hog meat and corn grits. Sofkee and blue dumplings.

Once, she said, they'd had nothing to eat but pumpkins for three days.

She'd used possum fat for candle tallow.

She remembered scary stories of men who killed their wives and got away with it. The women would be found in the creek or in the woods with their heads wedged between the rocks. Once there was a woman who killed her children. Her grandma's voice had been full of stories.

She was in a parade of her memories. That was what Indian Territory meant sometimes. It was a *looking back*.

Her grandma had spoke a combination of Creek and Cherokee and English. Her family had intermarried. She inherited mixed and erased bounderies, merging into one another. Her family wasn't on the Cherokee rolls, but bypassed and sidestepped the roll takers. When they had come around, or when someone asked their names, they said something else.

"*Cos-a-go*." (He isn't writing my name.)

"*Sos-a-go*." (He's scratching it.)

She said there were panthers then.

Her grandma was a Christian, but the other world moved for her too.

Her grandma's parents had slept in a wagon when they first came. Then they had a tent, a dugout, a sod house, and finally a cabin, full of smallpox, rain, mud, snakes, rodents.

They buried their dead in the yard.

Sometimes they had revivals that lasted for days. They were crazy with religion. Somewhere she had her grandma's Cherokee Bible.

She remembered her grandma had branded her goats so no one else would claim them. A little spirit sign. Something like she had on her truck.

She found three of the rocks that marked the corners of her grandma's place, but finally gave up on the fourth. To ignore her heritage was hard; to live in it was harder. She had wobbled between the two. She had feet in both worlds.

Why would she look back? What had any of them had? What was history other than a sadness that made her scratch her legs in the weeds and grasses where she sat? Wasn't it just more striving in an earlier form?

She had done what she could. Why couldn't she forgive herself?

Because then she'd have to forgive her parents.

She sat in the fieldweeds and grasses that was her grandma's place. She felt the long trail of her ancestors. It was a small, hard part of her that had to keep moving because it relieved her brokenness, her separateness.

Sometimes she didn't care where she was going as long as she was going.

She must have slept in the grass at her grandmother's old place. Even her dreams paraded.

She saw the wampum beads her grandma kept in her sewing basket.

Her grandmother's cane chair and quilted pillow.

She could feel them in her hands.

She could see her grandma pouring a sugar bowl of sugar into her coffee, and pouring a sip of the coffee into her saucer, and cutting a piece of piecrust, and dipping it in the sugared coffee in her saucer.

She saw her grandma tie her clothes to the line, or else the shirts and dresses would become birds and fly away.

When she shucked corn, the husks would become wings.

Ears of corn had flown into the wind.

Even elderberries had changed into birds and flew from the basket.

Sometimes the spirits were so thick, she couldn't walk from her house of an evening.

"I am part of several of them," her grandma had said.

She saw the brown paper she folded and the stacks of string. The twists of tobacco and fruit jars.

The road was a tongue. When she drove, she heard it talk to her truck.

When she got back to her house, she looked for the old Bible.

16

Ch   TEℎℎ   ᎤᏪᏉᏫᎤᎭ

tsani	igvyiyi	uwowelanvhi
John	first	written by him

ᎾᏍᎩ	**ᏗᏓᎴᏂᏍᎬ**	**ᏤᎮᎢ**,
nasgi	didalenisgv	tsehei
that	from the beginning	one that lived

ᎣᎦᏛᎦᏅᎯ,	**ᏦᏥᎦᏙᎵ**	**ᏦᎬᏔᏅᎯ**,	**ᎣᎯᎪᎲᎯ**
ogatvganvhi	tsotsigatoli	tsogvtanvhi	ogigohvhi
we have heard	our eyes	we used	what we saw

ᎠᎴ	**ᏦᎪᏰᏂ**	**ᎣᎦᏒᏂᎵᏙᎸᎯ**,	**ᎧᏃᎮᏛ**
ale	tsogoyeni	ogasvhnilidolvhi	kanohedv
and	our hands	what we touched	word

ᎬᏂᏛ-	**ᏄᎵᏍᏔᏅᎩ**,	**ᎠᎴ**	**ᎣᎩᎪᎲᎩ**,	**ᎣᏥᏃᎮᎭ**,
gvhnidv	nulistrngi	ale	ogigohvgi	otsinoheha
life	it happened	and	we saw	we are speaking of

ᎠᎵᏍᏆᏗᏍᎩ	**ᏂᎨᏒᎾ**	**ᏤᎮᎢ**,
alisgwadisgi	nigesvna	tsehei
that which ends	not	he lived

Ꮎ	**ᎣᎩᎪᎲᎯ**	**ᎠᎴ**	**ᎣᎦᏛᎦᏅᎯ**	**ᎢᏨᎾᏄᎪᏫᏎᎭ**,
na	ogigohvhi	ale	ogatvganvhi	itsvnanugowiseha
which	what we saw	and	what we heard	we are making known

ᎾᏍᏉ	**ᏂᎯ**	**ᎣᎦᏚᏓᏕᏭᏒᎢ**;	**ᎠᎦᏴᎵᎨᎢ**	**ᎠᎴ**	**ᎤᏪᏥ**
nasgwo	nihi	ogadudadewusv	agyvliegei	ale	uwetsi
also	you	woven together	elder	and	son

ᏥᏌ	**ᎦᎶᏁᏛ**.
tsiasa	galonedv
Jesus	Christ

17

"I feel like I'm a plate on a tablecloth pulled closer to the edge of the table," she sat in the cafe talking to Yellow Bud. "My father and mother're dead. My former husband's gone. Now my son's married. I don't know where I'm going either."

Yellow Bud had retired from his auto sales, repair, and paint business at the end of Muskogee Street. He was deciding what to do with his life as he ate his lunch.

"I feel like I live without half my heart, not knowing where the rest of it is." She called to the waitress for more ketchup for Yellow Bud. The bottle was nearly empty.

"Got too many enemies over the year," Yellow Bud explained, twisting a napkin around his stained knuckles. He always sat with the women as they talked. She had known his mother when he was a boy. His mother was gone now, but Yellow Bud still liked to talk with the women.

She noticed some of the customers stared at Yellow Bud as he ate. He must have noticed, though he didn't let them know.

"I'll set up in Eldon or Proctor or Westville."

"You ought to go someplace they haven't heard of you," she said.

"Maybe in Rogers, maybe someplace else," he said. "I might just go fishing."

Yes, there was a plate on the edge of the table and the next pull would spill her to the floor. It looked like Yellow Bud would topple too.

He paid his bill and tipped his hat to a man who scowled at him from a side booth.

There had been misunderstandings, she thought.

Confrontations.

Her family had a parade of them.

There was the parade of the health inspector through her cafe.

There was the parade of the earth across the sky.

Of planets around the sun.

She sat in the front window twirling a napkin around her hand and wondered what to do the rest of the evening when the noise of the cafe settled.

There had been old migration trails to this country.

There had been a parade of ships.

There had been a parade of boyfriends. They were widowers longing for their dead wives, or if they were divorced, they had children with a suckhole of problems. There had been a man who came into the cafe nearly every night. He was the father of one of her son's friends, but she suspected he gambled or drank. Sometimes she could tell about a man; she got a sense there was a reason he was unattached to anyone.

There was even a parade of trees as she drove to her house, but she was the one moving, not them. When she looked with parading eyes, even failure and setbacks were the fuel for more migrations, more parades across time. She'd gotten those eyes from her father, and would continue to see through them until the wheel of her will was stopped, and at last she would fall from the table and fly into the parade to the afterlife with her folded wings.

18

Even when the birds.

19

Another postcard from her former husband:

Poached Fish Pontiac
  Distance: 40 miles
  One 3/4 pound thick fillet of firm white fish
  3–4 tablespoons dry vermouth or white wine
  3 tablespoons minced shallots
  1 bay leaf
  Ground white pepper to taste
  Butter

At home or on the road, lay out a sheet of foil and butter it lightly. Place the fish on the foil, then tuck up the sides and sprinkle the vermouth or wine over the fish. Spread the shallots on top, then add the bay leaf, pepper, and a few dabs of butter. Close foil carefully and wrap tight.

Cooking time is approximately 45 minutes, check after 30 minutes if fish is in direct contact with the manifold.

Her former husband was always sending changes for the menu. He just was never around to actually make them. Therefore, the menu never changed.

She thought of recipes; she thought of spirit signs in the menu, in the butter.

Sometimes she would hear his voice. "If only you had a tongue like a butter knife."

"Tell the menu stories." A spirit said.

Had she ever felt the spirits in her cafe? She sat there in the dark another night after she closed.

She felt the long parade of food through the cafe.

The parade of customers.

The spirits with their masks on backwards. Were they coming or going? She couldn't see in the dark. One had a kerchief around his neck like Gene Autry, her girlhood hero, except Gene wasn't there for her either.

Spirits stood in the kitchen like they'd stood at her truck.

Even if her former husband walked in the door now, nothing would change.

20

At the powwow ground, the men were dancing w/ headdresses w/ spinners and rockers; they were dancing with yellow-jacket wings.

We come together, she thought, *our costumes fancy-dancing in vans and trucks.*

Janet Gillette had worked on her jingle dress all year, and she was going to jingle as she followed the women into the arena. *The strut, I want to strut, oh be humble, be humble,* she heard her daughter-in-law say. Janet's hair braided tight, she probably couldn't close her eyes at night.

She remembered when she thought the powwow was a place to find a boyfriend, or a cigarette. She remembered feeling left out at the powwow, as well as at school. Now the students she saw at the powwow were in their school's student government.

She saw her son watching Janet Gillette as she danced in the circle of women. He was always looking at her.

She remembered her father dancing.

She had to look backward, so she could see where she came from, so she could be in tune with tradition. It's why the spirits wore masks on the back of their heads.

But when she looked back, she also saw her father with eyes that saw no one but himself.

She watched the powwow dancers. If she danced, she would pound her feet, angry at the earth. She thought of the wind eroding the Arbuckle Anticline. She felt her own buckled layers pushed up from within.

"*Otsinoheha alisgwadisgi nigesvan.*" (We are speaking of that which ends not.)

She wondered if any of the men were watching her. She wasn't in traditional costume, but her shirt had silver studs across the back. She realized her self-centered thought, and put it aside. She tried to concentrate on the Great Spirit. The matter of alignment.

She got up from her lawn chair, and danced in the powwow circle, facing her anger, hurt, her sorrow and guilt. She felt them being pulled out of her like long, white, thick, flat ribbons.

She felt her determination to survive the details of running a cafe. She felt the beating of her heart alone in her chest. No, it wasn't alone. The drum walked with her, or with the half of her heart she felt, as her feet followed the sound of the drum in the clear powwow air. That was what *Indian Territory* meant. Survival. Or struggle for survival. Or retrieval. Or reckoning with what had passed. It had a movable meaning, depending where you were in the parade.

21

She was driving to her son's house for supper.

She'd had the name of *Redlands* in Cherokee painted on the cafe, just like the bank and hardware and other businesses in Tahlequah. She had called Yellow Bud out of hiding to paint it. Now she was running late, even for Indian time.

She saw the parade of autumn leaves. The burst of corn rows.

The white flash of clouds.

She felt a place within her as long as she was on the move.

Maybe, sometimes, women were the warriors of the world.